"You do

Katarina looked
shoulder on the
arms over his c
constraints of his sleeves.

"No."

She was shocked by the lack of hesitation in Alex's reply. "You've never even met him. How can you make that kind of judgment?"

"I don't like anyone who steals that smile from your face," he said without pause.

Katarina hesitated, momentarily baffled. Her heartbeat quickened, and she found herself breathing faster. "That kind of comment, Alex MacIntyre, could get you into a heap of trouble."

One side of his mouth curved into a resigned smile as he raised an eyebrow. "I think I already am."

Books by Carol Steward

Love Inspired

There Comes a Season #27
Her Kind of Hero #56
Courting Katarina #134

CAROL STEWARD

lives with her hero/husband of twenty years and three teenage children in Greeley, Colorado. When she isn't busy caring for preschoolers in her home, she keeps busy with the activities of her daughter and two sons, and with volunteer work for various organizations. A retired cake decorator, Carol enjoys camping, restoring antiques, tole-painting, needlework, gardening, traveling, sewing and collecting Noah's Ark items.

She loves to hear from readers. You may write to her at: Carol Steward, P.O. Box 5021, Greeley, CO 80631-0021.

Courting Katarina

STEEPLE HILL BOOKS

ISBN 0-373-87141-4

COURTING KATARINA

Printed in U.S.A.

Delight thyself in the Lord and He shall give you the desires of thine heart. Commit thy way unto the Lord, trust in Him, and He shall bring it to pass.
—*Psalms* 37:4,5

Thanks to Bob, and his wife, Vicki,
for their help in understanding the extraordinary
demands of smoke jumpers and wildland
firefighters. What a truly heroic line of work
and special people, to carry it out year after year.

To my brother, Randy,
who doesn't know a stranger.

And to my sisters, Mindy, Cathy and Cindy, for
inspiring me to write a series about that incredible,
indelible relationship only sisters can understand.

Chapter One

Katarina Berthoff dabbed the tears collecting in the corners of her eyes. Her sister was married. After eleven years, Kevin and Emily had *finally* gotten it right. Pictures had been taken, the reception was running smoothly and her bridesmaid's obligations were finished. Until the bride and groom left for their honeymoon and Katarina began to take care of their newly adopted four-year-old, she was free to relax with the other guests.

Laughter and the murmur of voices from the crowd created a constant echo in her ear, so she discreetly removed her hearing aid, placed it in the case and dropped it into her purse. She hated to wear it in large gatherings. She'd pay nearly any price, even this deafness, to avoid the drone from all the background noise, and the headache that always followed. She didn't need anything else to deal with today. *One of these days, I'm going to have enough money to buy one of the new models that won't be such a problem.*

Bypassing the assortment of cheeses and luncheon meats at the banquet table, Katarina studied the chafing dishes filled with mushrooms, meatballs and tiny quiches. She stopped at the elaborately decorative platter of fruit and filled her plate with melon, strawberries and grapes, then studied a pale yellow star-shaped fruit.

A deep masculine voice interrupted. "Katarina?"

She turned and nearly dropped her plate. There stood Alex MacIntyre. Her heart skipped a beat and she felt her cheeks flush. "Hello. We meet again, finally." With all the last-minute decorations and reception preparations to take care of, Katarina hadn't had a chance to visit with anyone at the rehearsal the night before. She'd met the groom's brother only once, at Kevin and Emily's first engagement party eight years ago. The college graduate had made quite an impression on her as a high school senior. When Kevin and Emily broke their engagement, Katarina had lost hope she would ever see Alex again.

He nodded. "It's been a long time. When Kevin told me who you were last night, I could hardly believe you're the same woman I met eight years ago. You've…changed."

And you *haven't.* Alex was even more attractive than she remembered. Suddenly overcome by a gamut of perplexing emotions, Katarina glanced quickly away, then back to him. Did he approve of the changes? "Do I hear 'thankfully' in that remark, Alex?"

He smiled in a leisurely way, looking a bit chagrined. "It's definitely meant as a compliment. I wasn't sure you'd even remember me."

Like I could actually forget those gorgeous blue eyes? Not a chance. "It amazes me how much you and Kevin look alike." When Alex had come to Springville a few weeks earlier to help run Kevin's business after Kevin's accident, Emily had wasted no time informing Katarina of Alex's availability.

Though already dating someone, Katarina had to admit she'd been curious to see if Alex had changed. Only for the better, she realized.

Now she wished she'd taken time to meet him before he returned to his own job and life, wherever that might be.

Alex's smile was white against his bronzed skin. "Don't hold it against me—that's where the similarities end. Care to sit with the wild bunch?"

Katarina furrowed her eyebrows. "The wild bunch?"

"Any time you get the entire MacIntyre clan together, it's chaos." He tipped his head toward the table nearest the cake, where his siblings appeared to be seated. "I'd love for you to join us."

Love for her to join him? She couldn't resist. No wonder her sisters had nicknamed her "the heart specialist.'' Despite her older sister, Emily, actually becoming a doctor, Kat's honorary title remained. When it came to matters of the heart, she was a romantic in the purest form.

She felt color flush her cheeks as she recalled the crush she'd had on Alex MacIntyre—business major, football star and all-around nice guy. She glanced at the happy faces around the table. Did she dare tempt herself twice in one lifetime? *I'm practically engaged. There's no harm in making friends with my sister's new family. Besides, after the honeymoon Alex will return to his life. No harm done.*

She set her plate on the table and Alex immediately pulled out her chair. She chose her seat so that he would sit on the side of her good ear.

Kevin's twin sisters and another brother were catching up with each other's lives, laughing and having a good time when she sat down. Alex waited for the chatter to quiet, then went around the table making introductions. By turning her head slightly, Katarina didn't think she would miss anything.

Alex reminded his family that Katarina had been instrumental in pulling together the wedding decorations at the church and the reception with less than a week's notice. Everyone showered her with adoration. She wanted to fade into the woodwork. True, she had a knack for decorating or she wouldn't have celebrated her fourth year as owner of Kat's Kreations. Yet the attention her talent received still made her uncomfortable. ''The credit really goes to Emily.

She and Kevin picked it all out. I just put it together.''

"Kevin helped?" The laughter roared, and Katarina realized they probably couldn't imagine their brother in a flower shop, let alone that he cared to help with wedding plans. Alex smiled apologetically. "Forgive us, Katarina. We haven't been together much in recent years to see this side of Kevin.''

Still Mr. Nice Guy.

She shifted in her chair and felt as if the seat was sinking beneath her. Katarina's slim-fitting dress bound her legs tighter, and she raised herself slightly to pull the fabric loose, then sat back down.

With a loud snap, the chair collapsed, and Katarina slid as if on a chute under the table. All she could see were legs. And feet. The tablecloth draped itself over her shoulder, and Katarina ducked her head under the table completely, welcoming the shelter from her embarrassment.

She tried to turn over and crawl out, but her spike heel caught inside her skirt. She was stuck.

I can't believe this. She squirmed the other way, and made matters worse. Why did this have to happen today, of all days? Katarina closed her eyes. Taunting voices from her childhood haunted her. *Klutzy Katarina.*

Beyond the veil of linens she could see pieces of the plastic chair in a tangled heap on the ground.

Katarina relished the haven from her humiliation. At least she was away from probing gazes.

Feet scuttled around, concerned faces replaced the legs. She saw mouths move and she covered her face, oblivious to what they were saying. She didn't want their pity or their help. She only wanted to hide.

Katarina again tried to untie herself from the human knot of her twisted body. She rested her forehead on her knees, wrapped her arms around her head and began to giggle nervously.

Only she could get herself into such a ridiculous situation.

Her sister's new in-laws would probably agree with the playground nickname, "Klutzy Katarina." Suddenly she was a sickly child again, wishing the jeers of her classmates would stop. "Go away. Just go away," she whispered. When Katarina opened her eyes, she saw the kitchen doorway just past the table and pulled herself forward. If she could just scoot to the kitchen without drawing any more attention…

The dress tied her legs together like a mermaid's.

Alex's younger brother lifted the tablecloth in front of her and took hold of her ankle. Then her calf. Startled, Katarina pulled back. "Just leave me alone," she begged. So much for a silent escape.

"I've got her." A strong arm wrapped around her waist from behind and slid her out from under the table and into the spotlight. "Are you deaf?"

She looked over her shoulder to see the sun-bleached hair of her handsome rescuer. Alex. Trying to fend off the memories of children's cruel teasing, she forced herself to focus on him. He didn't know she *was* truly deaf in one ear. And only a select few knew the degree of her hearing loss in her "good" ear. Katarina laughed. "Silly me, I must have forgotten my hearing aid today." Struggling to free her foot, she felt Alex hoist her off the ground. "Wait!"

Before she could explain, he let go and she fell against him. "My heel is caught."

The warmth of his hands pressed into her upper arms. "Sorry, why didn't you say something? Here, have a seat while I try to do something." He helped her over to the chair. Alex knelt on one knee and struggled with her shoe. "You did a dandy job snagging that heel somewhere in there. Maybe we should take it off?"

"Excuse me?" Her voice squeaked.

"The shoe." As he tugged, she heard the satin rip, and her leg straightened.

He held up her pump. "I'm sorry about the dress."

Stunned, Katarina stood and turned to look at the tear, then took her shoe from him. No one had ever flustered her like this. The words caught in her throat.

"I'll replace the dress." One eyebrow rose as Alex looked at the rip.

It's over. Just laugh, Katarina. That always helps.
"Don't worry about it."

Emily rushed over, white lace flowing behind her.
"Are you okay, Kat?"

"I'll be fine." She twisted to the side to examine
the damage to the dress. "I wondered how this
would look with a slit." She lifted her foot and
twirled on the other so the bride could see, noting
that Alex also watched. Then she straightened the
dress and slipped her other shoe off. Glancing up,
Katarina saw a smile teasing Emily's lips. "I don't
want to hear about this again."

The bride excused herself from her guests to help
Katarina and led the way down the hall to the bride's
dressing room. Emily's concern was genuine. "You
are okay, aren't you, Kat?" Once inside, Emily
could no longer restrain her laughter.

"Other than my bruised ego, I'm fine."

A light tap on the door, followed by their younger
sister's voice, startled Katarina. "Is there a damsel
in distress in here?" Lisa opened the door just
enough to slip inside with Katarina's other outfit.

The facade of Katarina's humor faded. She tossed
both shoes into her bag and sighed. "Why do these
things always happen to me?"

Lisa turned Katarina around and unzipped the
gown, then helped tug it over her shoulders. "What
things? It's not your fault the chair broke into smith-
ereens."

Katarina buttoned the flowered rayon skirt at her

waist, pulled the camisole over her head, then slipped into the coordinating sweater. "Like when I fainted at the all-school concert in sixth grade. Like tripping over the base in kickball. Like dropping my brand-new hearing aid into my punch at the prom. Why is it always me…Klutzy Katarina?"

"This isn't the same, Kat. Your ear infections were to blame for most of that." Emily smiled as she gave her sister a hug. "If you wanted to meet Alex, why didn't you just ask? We'd be glad to set the two of you up."

"No, thank you." Her sister's medical explanation soothed her ego, and she felt the fear subside. "That's not the issue, and I don't want to hear about this again."

Her sisters' smiles returned. "Well, you can dream on. This is a classic. The tall, rugged, single and not to mention drop-dead-gorgeous hero hauls you, the 'heart specialist,' out from under the table, stands you up and you collapse into his arms." They giggled harder.

Lisa and Emily did a poor imitation of the accident. "You looked like a flamingo balancing on one foot," Lisa added.

Quelling her own laughter, Katarina crossed her arms over her chest and glared at her sisters until they quieted. "Ha ha ha." Though she tried to remain cross, just the sight of their fake restraint made her see the humor of the entire situation.

"Why did it have to happen in front of Alex, though?" she whispered, shaking her head.

The room turned silent. Realization hit Lisa. "Ah, yes, *Alex.*"

Katarina placed the bridesmaid dress on the hanger and zipped it, then turned to help Lisa and Emily with the wedding dress and veil. "I mean, it's been eight years since I had that childish crush on him, and of course I'm long over *that,* but still…"

"Of course," both sisters said simultaneously with mirroring smiles.

"Come on, don't do this. I'm as good as engaged to…to…"

"Ron?" Lisa suggested.

"Of course, to Ron," Katarina snapped.

Emily groaned. "Oh, please, Kat. You've been 'engaged' so many times we quit counting. Don't try to convince us that you're serious about marrying *Ron.* Need I point out you just moved four hundred miles away from him?" The bride slipped the green dress over her head.

"This will only be my second official engagement. Besides, the move is temporary." She looked at them, putting her hands up in front of her. "It's all part of a logical, strategic plan. Ron understands my need for financial security."

"Strategy, my foot. Admit it—the thought of settling down with him bores you to death!"

Katarina looked at Emily—with her hands on her

hips—and tried to argue the well-made point. "As does the idea of chasing a man almost ten years older than myself, Dr. Know-it-all."

"Alex is only nine years older, Katarina."

"Close enough. Needless to say, I discovered that mistake with fiancé number one. I made it this far without a father in my life. I certainly don't need some older man to act as a substitute now."

Just the mention of the father who had abandoned his three little girls sobered them all. Katarina looked at her sisters. "I'm sorry. I didn't need to bring that up today. I really didn't mean to. Open mouth, insert foot."

Lisa remained silent.

As usual, Emily was the first to forgive and console the younger two sisters. "It's okay, Kat. You can't have a wedding without missing the father of the bride."

A loud knock resounded through the room. "Mrs. MacIntyre," came the groom's seductive voice. "Are you ready to toss the bouquet?"

Emily opened the door and greeted her husband. "Don't forget, you have to toss the garter, too."

Kevin gave his wife a lingering kiss. "Then we'd better get back to our guests." Kevin looked at Katarina as she passed through the door. "You okay?"

Katarina looked at Kevin, suddenly seeing Alex instead. She blinked the image away, then set her shoes on the floor and stepped into the flats as she walked. "I'm just dandy, thanks."

Chapter Two

Alex washed shaving cream from the windows of Kevin's hunter-green pickup with the wand at the car wash while his new nephew and the best man, watched.

Bryan looked at his watch. "We'd better hurry—they should be ready to leave soon. I think Alex got it all off, don't you, Ricky?"

"Yup, looks pretty clean."

The best man laughed. "You're too kind, Alex," Bryan said as he opened the door. Ricky jumped into the cab of the truck. "Do you know how many newlyweds Kevin has sent off for their honeymoon in a decorated car?"

Alex slid the wand into the tube and flipped the switch off. "Nice has nothing to do with it." Alex winked. "I don't want to take any chances of damaging the paint. I don't need a repair bill hanging over me. Where are they going for their honeymoon?''

The men climbed into the truck and closed the doors. ''You don't actually think he's going to tell me, do you?''

Alex turned the key in the ignition and pulled forward. ''Well…'' He paused, eyeing the orphaned little boy his brother and new sister-in-law had officially adopted at the end of the wedding ceremony. After all these years, it was a shock to see one of the MacIntyre brothers actually married. ''Surely they told someone where they can be reached, didn't they?''

Silently Bryan raised his eyebrows and shrugged.

As if the four-year-old understood, he interjected, ''Auntie Kat is 'sitting me, Bryan, 'member? And Uncle Alex promised to take me for pizza. Can Katarina come with us? It wouldn't be nice to leave her home alone.''

Alex wanted more than anything to ignore the question. He was most likely the last person Katarina Berthoff wanted to spend time with after he'd snapped at her. It wasn't like him to be so short of patience, but he'd tried to find out what had happened, and how he could help. She'd ignored him. How could he help if she wouldn't talk to him?

Of course, then he'd hauled her out from under the table like some brute and embarrassed her. ''Well, Ricky, we'll have to see how your aunt Katarina feels about that first.'' He certainly wouldn't mind a dinner with his sister-in-law's charming sister, yet he wasn't sure she'd agree.

"She might get lonely."

The two men looked at one another and laughed, obviously of the same opinion that Katarina would probably relish a few minutes of solitude after two days alone with the talkative little boy. Alex pulled into the driveway that led to the exclusive restaurant perched on a bluff with a view of town. Emily and Kevin exited the Dutch-style building and looked around for the truck. Alex paused for a minute, enjoying the momentary look of panic on his brother's face.

Alex slowly pulled forward and stopped just in front of the bride and groom, opening his door just as Emily invited all eligible women to gather for the bouquet toss. Alex unbuckled Ricky's seat belt. "What a ridiculous tradition," he muttered. "They don't actually believe catching a bouquet can predict the next bride-to-be, do they?"

Bryan chuckled, "Need I remind you, Emily caught Laura's bouquet merely five months ago?"

"Coincidence." Alex tried to ignore the shrill screams of excitement and pleas for Emily to throw the wildflowers. As she did, he stole a quick glance at Katarina. When had the gangly teenager turned into an alluring young woman?

Alex tugged at the knot of his tie and unfastened his collar button, then looked up. The wildflowers were caught in the tree. On the other side of the truck, his brother jumped up and knocked them loose.

Alex batted the bouquet away when it dropped in front of him. The screaming resumed as the bundle glided directly into Katarina Berthoff's hands.

She stared at it as if it were a kiss of death instead of a prediction of marriage. He couldn't help but smile as Lisa, the bride's youngest sister, arched her eyebrows and gave Katarina a hug.

Wishing he could crawl back into the truck and drive away, Alex walked over to his youngest brother and repeated his earlier question. "They don't actually believe this stuff works, do they?"

Adam laughed. "Doesn't really matter, does it? Takes two to tango, and I've had enough toes stepped on to stay off the dance floor permanently."

"Those city women are what made you run back to Granddaddy's ranch?"

His brother looked indignant. "You must be kidding. That ranch has been my dream forever. You should know that. But there's one thing a guest ranch doesn't need. Women."

Alex chuckled. "Give it time, and you'll be singing a different tune."

He glanced at Katarina again, imagining her in a white lace gown, holding her own bouquet. Would the owner of Kat's Kreations put together as fancy a wedding for herself?

Adam's voice pulled Alex from his daydream. "So, brother, what's kept you from tying that proverbial knot? Will we be adding one more plate to the Christmas table this year? Or are we going to hold strong to our bachelorhood?''

Alex looked around at the variety of couples in the crowd. If he were only in a different line of business, the first thing he'd do was find himself a wife and start a family. After all, he was thirty-five already. Where had the time gone?

As long as he was fighting fires, he wasn't husband material. Six-month stretches away from home were no way to make a marriage work. No way to raise a family. Not for him, anyway. In his eight years as a smokejumper, he'd seen more marriages fall apart than stay together. ''Don't count me in for Christmas. Who knows where I'll be by then.''

''Bachelors, gather around,'' called Kevin. ''Your turn.'' With much ado, Kevin seated Emily in the wicker chair, retrieved the garter from his wife's leg, turned around and tossed it over his shoulder.

Adam slapped Alex on the back. ''It's headed right for you, bro. Better run quick.''

Alex shook his head and laughed as he saw the blue-and-white lace sailing directly toward him. ''No way! You've got the wrong guy.'' *The last thing I need is a woman to complicate my life right now.* ''Wrong guy,'' he repeated, staring at the frilly garter in his hand.

The competing bachelors gathered around. With Adam in the lead, they not so gently ''guided'' him to Katarina. "Now you put it on her," Adam explained.

Katarina's eyes grew huge and the color drained from her cheeks. Someone gave Alex a blatant shove and he stopped short of running into her. He looked at Katarina and shrugged. "Do you mind?"

She leaned forward, lifting her ear closer to his mouth. Wildflowers. She smelled like a forest before a fire. Was it the bouquet in her hand, or some carefully concocted perfume? Or his imagination? He didn't dare explore the answer.

"What did you say? I didn't hear you over all the noise." Katarina's voice held a mixture of shyness and teasing. There was something warm and enchanting about her. If he didn't get this over with, the crowd wouldn't give him a minute of peace for the rest of the afternoon. Katarina was trouble with a capital *T*. He could tell that already.

She was too young. Too sensitive. Too beautiful to be alone all summer long while he jumped out of planes, wondering where the next forest fire would take him. Worried that he might not make it home at all.

He wouldn't be the man responsible for placing worry lines on that innocent face.

"I asked if you mind?" he said into her ear, inhaling deeply. It was definitely her perfume.

Katarina nodded slightly, obviously too startled by the suggestion to offer any objection. She paused, lifted her chin and met his gaze. He nodded, and she sat down. Her flowered skirt flowed around her feet and dusted the ground.

Alex knelt on one knee and swallowed the lump in his throat. His heart raced as if he'd just bailed out of the Twin Otter at fifteen hundred feet. He'd take jumping into a forest fire over this any day.

She lifted the edge of her skirt little more than an inch above her ankle, challenging him to go through with it. The crowd roared, hooting and hollering suggestions. He had no intention of following any of them. He just wanted this to be over.

As he slid the garter over Katarina's ankle, he watched a dim flush return to her pale and beautiful face. He stopped at her calf, noting the heated gaze that passed between them. Trying to mirror the light mood of the crowd, he forced a smile.

"You're off the hook," Katarina leaned close to say. The glint of humor shone in her blue eyes as she tucked a stray blond hair behind her ear. "I'm as good as engaged already," she added with a coy smile.

"And what makes you think I want to be *on* the hook?"

Chapter Three

The wedding festivities ended and the family dispersed. Alex watched Katarina with mixed emotions. She and her sister gathered the last of the flower vases from the tables and placed them in a crate. He should have his head examined for flirting with her.

What exactly does "good as engaged" mean, anyway? He pushed the question aside and concentrated on figuring out a way to make peace with the bride's sister. He strolled over and stopped in front of her. "Can I carry that to the car for you?"

"I can manage." Katarina stacked the crate on a flat box, then deliberately turned away. "Lisa, would you find Mom and Ricky? We're ready to go." Katarina's voice held a tone of defiance.

He had obviously made her plenty mad. Who

knew exactly what it was this time? There were more options than hamburgers on a fast-food menu.

Lisa eyed the load her sister had prepared. "You sure you can handle all that?"

Katarina hoisted the teetering load off the table. "I do it all the time. No problem."

Her feistiness reminded him of a kitten—delicate, adorable and determined. She rested her chin on the edge of the crate to stabilize it.

"Okay, I'll be right back," Lisa said, eyeing Alex. Lisa hesitated, shrugged her shoulders, then disappeared around the corner.

Sidestepping to get out of Katarina's way, Alex matched her gait step for step. "There's no reason for you to carry all that. I'll be glad to help."

"I don't need any help. But thanks anyway."

Despite her protests, he took the crate of wildflowers from the stack and waited for her to lead the way. "I'd rather carry it than clean up the mess when all this crystal breaks." He took a deep breath and realized the wildflowers weren't aromatic. Certainly not the inspiration for Katarina's perfume.

"It would have been perfectly fine." Katarina marched past him, her flowered skirt billowing in the breeze. She stepped outside, and her hair glistened in the sunshine.

She shoved the box into the back of her station wagon. Alex set the crate into the one empty space left. The remains of Katarina's gown hung in the back seat.

It wasn't his fault, he reminded himself. Nonetheless, he felt responsible. "I hope your dress isn't ruined." He reached into his back pocket and pulled out his wallet. "Here, at least let me pay to have it mended."

She laughed softly. "Trust me, it's beyond repair." She stood straight and met his gaze. "However, nothing's ever a total loss." Katarina waved her hand, as if to shoo away his guilt and his wallet. She reached into the car, grabbed a box marked Cake Top and moved it to a more secure spot. "The dress will be much more practical once I shorten it, anyway. I can always use the scraps of fabric for my dolls." She rambled on while rearranging supplies inside the car.

Alex watched Katarina tuck a strand of her chin-length hair behind her ear. He could almost imagine smelling her perfume, and took another whiff, disappointed that he couldn't pick up the scent again. As Katarina chattered on about possibilities for that piece of fabric, she almost convinced him he'd done her a great favor in tearing the gown.

"I hope I didn't embarrass you today. I wasn't sure how to get out of that ridiculous garter charade." He chuckled. "Who makes up these traditions, anyway?"

"These traditions are fun, for one thing." A momentary flash of disappointment crossed her face. "And once in a while the predictions actually come true. Just look at Emily and Kevin." She slammed the hatch closed.

"What did I say this time?" Why it mattered that he understand why she was so irritated he didn't know. He'd be gone in a few weeks and they'd probably never see each another again. He shrugged his shoulders. "I'm sorry."

"For what? Ruining a perfectly beautiful day and turning a joyful celebration into a circus?" She choked out the words, then cleared her throat and forced a smile. "Don't think another thing of it. It was a no-win situation. We survived."

Though he'd meant the comment as a joke—to make light of the awkward situation—she'd taken his ridicule seriously. Couldn't she see that he'd been kidding? It was impossible to deny his attraction to the icy-blue-eyed, honey-blond woman who could brighten any day with her cheerfulness. Which made it even worse that he was the one person who'd taken her smile away. "I was joking."

Katarina let out a soft sigh of frustration. She must have had a long week. She looked up at him and wrinkled her nose as she squinted from the bright sun. "I suppose I should apologize for seeming less than grateful for your help earlier. That broken chair certainly wasn't your fault." She rushed through the statement and turned away, obviously uncomfortable with him for some reason.

"Don't mention it." He didn't want to discuss that again. "Well," he said with regret, "I guess I should just get right to the point. I have a small favor to ask.'' If the woman didn't want him around, so be it. He needed to get back to Kevin's house. ''My brother and sisters leave in the morning, and we'd all like to spend some time with Ricky before they leave.'' He explained their impromptu barbecue, terribly uncomfortable with not inviting her. ''I'll make sure I have Ricky back home in time for bed.''

''I'm sure that would be okay with Kevin and Emily. Mom and Lisa need to be in Denver to catch their flights in a couple of hours, so I'll have him change clothes and bring him right over.''

Lisa ran out of the building and nearly tripped on her bridesmaid gown. ''Ricky's in a tree and can't get down!''

Alex hurried after Lisa. ''Where are they?''

Katarina closed up the car. ''Boy, is this day going downhill fast,'' she muttered. She quickly caught up to them. ''Why did Mom let him climb a tree?''

Lisa led the way past a tall hedge of lilacs around the park's perimeter. ''Mom said he needed to run off some energy. She took him to the playground. Apparently he's a monkey. Before she could stop him, Ricky was above her head. Need I remind you that we have to leave in an hour?''

Katarina shook her head. ''I don't need a reminder, or another lecture....''

Lisa hiked her dress up to her knees, struggling

to keep up with Alex's long stride. "Maybe we should call the fire department."

Katarina stopped. "Good grief, how big is the tree?"

Alex pulled his tuxedo jacket off as he walked, and tossed it to Katarina. "Here, hold this for me."

She looked at him wide-eyed. "What are you doing?"

"I plan to get our nephew out of that tree, before this day gets any worse. We'll get him down, don't worry. No need to call anyone yet."

Before she could argue, Alex handed her his rented shirt, tie and cummerbund.

Katarina watched as Alex approached the huge maple where her mother stood. Katarina's hands covered her mouth and she let out a small squeal. Ricky was nearly as high as a second-story window. "Oh, no."

Alex placed his hands on his hips and looked up. He spoke to the four-year-old in a deep and calming voice. "How you doing, Ricky?"

"He won't talk to me anymore," her mother answered. "I think he finally realized how high he is. He hasn't moved in several minutes."

Alex acknowledged Mrs. Berthoff's comments. His eyes remained fixed on Ricky. "Do you want me to come get you?"

Katarina tried to quell the quickening of her pulse as she admired Alex's control. His voice was gentle. Reassuring. Confident.

Ricky nodded. His knuckles were white as he clung to the small branches. Alex looked at the tree and reached up to the lowest limb.

Lisa squealed.

Katarina grabbed his arm. "You can't go up there. Wait. Let us call for help."

"I'll have him down before they can even get here. Don't worry. I do this all the time." He placed his hand on hers, and her heart skipped a beat. "Just in case, you can send up a little prayer."

"You rescue little boys all the time?" Katarina couldn't help wanting to know more about Alex MacIntyre. Even if she shouldn't.

"Not exactly. But don't worry."

"What exactly does 'not exactly' mean?"

"I'll explain later."

Katarina felt the strength in his hand and let out a sigh. The look in his blue eyes was of total confidence. "God, please bring both Alex and Ricky down safely."

He patted her hand and locked his gaze with hers. There was a tingle in the pit of her stomach. *Did I really say that out loud?*

"Thank you." His deep voice faded. "Now leave it in His hands. I'll be back down in just a bit."

Stunned back to reality, Katarina whispered to her sister and mother, "He makes it sound like a walk up the stairs." Pulling her gaze off Alex, she looked at her nephew's short legs straddling the branch, his arms wrapped around it with equal intensity. "Here comes Uncle Alex, Ricky." Katarina watched Alex climb the huge old tree with finesse. "What in the world do you do for a living?"

He paused a minute and studied the tree. "Fight forest fires." He had one more branch to go before he could reach the little boy. "I'm a smokejumper. Wish I had my boots and spurs right now." Just as he said it, his foot slipped off the branch.

"A-A-Alex!" She covered her eyes and waited to hear limbs breaking from his fall.

"I'm fine."

Katarina peeked between her fingers, then slowly removed her hands. Alex pulled himself up and leaned against the tree trunk. He secured his right leg on the branch below Ricky, and the left one on the next closest limb. Alex wrapped his hand around Ricky's ankle. "Okay, Ricky, I'm going to hold your leg and I want you to slide closer to me."

Ricky didn't move.

Katarina waited impatiently for a response. "Ricky, you need to help Uncle Alex. Okay?" Her voice quivered. Katarina clutched Alex's tuxedo and shirt even tighter, praying the frightened little boy would listen. *Please, God. Don't let anything happen to them.*

Ricky tried to stand up. Katarina gasped.

"Sit down, Ricky," Alex said calmly. "It's okay, I have hold of you. I won't let you fall."

Katarina tried to keep the panic from her voice,

just as Alex did. "Just scoot backward to Alex on your bottom." She took a deep breath and held it.

Slowly, Ricky moved.

Alex coaxed the youngster closer and took hold of his hand. He helped Ricky turn around, then wrapped the boy in his muscled embrace. "There, that wasn't so hard, was it?"

She felt her heart beating and she took a deep breath. That was only half the problem. Now they both had to get down.

Alex was calm, collected and in control. A take-charge kind of guy. Not her type. The last thing she wanted was someone trying to replace the father she never had. If her own father hadn't been able to stick around for the long haul, why would any other man?

Clinging to Ricky, Alex allowed the child to calm down before proceeding. What a picture the two made. Tough and tender. Alex was built lean and solid, yet gentle as a teddy bear. She didn't even want to think about what her sisters could make of her reaction.

"Alex?" Her voice was still shaky despite her efforts to keep it in control. He looked at her, and she silently pleaded for him to come down.

He nodded, as if he understood what she wanted to say. "You ready to get out of here, Ricky?"

"Yep."

"Okay, you just hang on tight to me."

"Like a baby monkey?"

"Sure, like a baby monkey," Alex agreed.

Ricky wrapped his legs around Alex's waist and clamped his hands together behind Alex's neck. Alex imitated a chimpanzee. "Ooo. Ooo. Eee. Eee. Eee. Aaa. Aaa."

When they reached the lowest branch, Alex wrapped one arm around Ricky's waist, then jumped. Ricky laughed. Katarina swept the little boy into her arms and gave him a huge hug. "I'm so glad you're okay."

He just giggled. "Uncle Alex is funny."

She set Ricky on the ground, stood and turned to Alex. "Funny? Well, I guess the trauma is over for Ricky, anyway. Thank you." Katarina looked at Alex's bare chest. "You have a few cuts." She started to touch one, then backed away, surprised by what she'd nearly done.

"I won't break," he said, grinning. He looked at the scrapes and wiped the drip of blood away. "Nothing major."

Naomi Berthoff stepped up. "Thank you, Alex. I'm sorry. I didn't think he'd be able to get into the tree, let alone climb so high."

"I wouldn't have thought so either, Mrs. Berthoff." He took Ricky's hand. "I hope Ricky won't try that again."

The little boy nodded silently.

Lisa patted Ricky's head. "I hate to break in, you monkeys, but we need to leave. Thank you, Alex." She paused and looked at Katarina, as if tempted to say something else. "We sure appreciate your help."

"Glad I could be of service." Alex reached his hand out to Katarina.

She froze.

"I'll take the tux now."

Katarina looked at the clothes she'd clung to, and handed them to Alex. "Oh, sorry, I forgot I had them."

His lips curved into a smile and Katarina felt her face flush.

He looked down and examined his pants for damage. "Guess you have more fabric for that collection of yours."

She smiled stiffly and handed him the bundle in her arms. "I'll bring Ricky over in a while?"

"Sure. And if you're not busy, feel free to join us."

"I am, but thanks for the invitation."

Chapter Four

Ricky bounded up the front steps toward Alex. Behind him, his sister's kids ran up the stairs screaming, chased by Alex's brother, Adam. Laughter echoed from the beamed ceiling. Ricky stopped, his eyes opened wide, then he turned around and dived into the folds of Katarina's skirt.

"Maybe this isn't such a good idea," Alex whispered.

Katarina spoke softly to Ricky and gave him a hug. She had obviously been around the child quite a bit. He clutched her leg as she stood up again. "This isn't like him," she whispered back, "but then, he has had a lot of changes in his life these past few weeks. I guess I should have thought of that."

He didn't want to force them to stay, yet he hoped he could coax his nephew to give them all a chance to get to know one another. Alex squatted. "Ricky, I'd sure like for you to meet the rest of your aunts and uncles. And you even have some cousins now. They're just your age." Alex reached out his hand and waited for the frightened child to respond. "Would you like to meet them?"

Ricky peered out from the fabric and pulled it across his face again, a mischievous grin on his face.

Alex chuckled. "I see he takes after his shy aunt Katarina."

Her cheeks turned pink. Trying to free Ricky from her skirt, Katarina blurted out another option. "Maybe I should stay. Would that be okay with you, Ricky?" She looked up with those bright blue eyes. "That is, if your family wouldn't mind."

Alex stifled his pleasure. Ricky wasn't the only one apprehensive about being there. And he didn't want to scare either of them away. "We wouldn't mind at all." He tore his gaze from Katarina. "What do you think, Ricky?"

The little boy nodded and grabbed Alex's outstretched hand, reaching out with the other for Katarina. "C'mon, Auntie Kat."

Alex led the way through Kevin's house to the backyard. Away from the noise inside, Ricky seemed more like his usual spunky self. "Come see the zebro."

"The zebra?" she repeated, puzzled.

She looked at Alex, and he shrugged his shoulders.

Katarina looked around the yard. He could see that sparkle in her eyes. She'd figured out what Ricky meant, and was now making a game of it.

She looked up into the maple tree and shook her head. "I don't see any zebras."

Ricky pointed to the object and giggled. "See, it's a zebro. An' Kevin, my new daddy, put a swing in it, too. C'mon." The little boy took hold of Katarina's hand and dragged her past the barbecue grill, past the picnic table full of glasses and food.

Alex followed, playing along with the ruse, as he, too, figured out the mystery. "Ricky, there is no such thing as a zebra with a swing inside."

"Yes, sir! See?" He pointed to the ivy-covered gazebo and pulled Katarina inside.

"Oh, a gazebo. Can you say ga-ze-bo?" Katarina's smile was warm and enthusiastic.

"Ga-ze-bro," Ricky repeated confidently.

Katarina praised his efforts. "Very good. Come here and try out the porch swing with me." She sat down and pulled her nephew onto the seat beside her.

Alex sat next to them and rested his arm on the back of the bench, wishing suddenly that they were alone. The thought surprised him. Katarina was attractive, and also spoken for. Even if she wasn't, with his life up in the air, he was in no position to set his sights on any woman.

His loneliness had nothing to do with Katarina, or coming home to help his brother run his construction company. Katarina wasn't just some woman he'd like to see a few times. They were practically related. He didn't need to complicate things. It would only make it that much more awkward to be around each other. After all, they were bound to be invited to the same family gatherings in the future.

He listened to Ricky and Katarina joking around. She had a contagious laugh, and the two fed off each other. Though the sound brought a smile to his lips, Alex was struck with an uncommon feeling of regret.

Adam bellowed over the crowd, "Burgers are ready."

Alex touched Katarina's shoulder. "You two ready for a bite?" Her contagious giggles came to an immediate stop, while Ricky's continued.

"I'm not hungry, but thanks, anyway. You two can go ahead without me." She pushed herself from the swing and went across the gazebo to the window on the other side.

Uncertain what had startled her so, Alex suggested Ricky help him fix his plate.

As she watched Alex lift Ricky to his shoulders, Katarina's mind drifted. How easy it had been to let the mood of the day carry her away with the relaxing sway of the swing, the soft voice of her sister's brother-in-law and the coziness of sharing a gazebo with a handsome man and an equally adorable child.

Just watching Alex, she had no doubts he'd make a wonderful father. Why hadn't he married? He seemed nice, considerate, and his looks certainly wouldn't stand in the way.

"Katarina?" Alex looked right at her.

She blinked, suddenly aware that she'd been staring. "What?" Why in the world was she daydreaming about Alex MacIntyre? A take-charge man didn't fit into her plans.

Ricky dangled over Alex's shoulder like a sack of flour, squealing with delight. "I'm going to take Ricky to meet everyone. You sure you don't want to come?"

She tipped her head toward the window and shook her head. "I think I'll just wait here. You two seem to be doing fine."

Alex swung Ricky to the ground. A smile teased Alex's lips. "No hiding out allowed. After all, you're part of the family, too." Then they were gone.

She watched as Alex and Ricky hugged Alex's mother. Ricky met his twin aunts, Elizabeth and Susan, their husbands and Susan's children, then devoured his supper.

A while later, Katarina ventured back to the group seated at the picnic table. Alex pulled up another chair and discreetly tested it before allowing Katarina to sit. She blushed, surprised that no one else seemed to notice what he'd done. He brought her a tall glass of lemonade, then sat next to her.

For the second time that day she wondered why

Alex was paying her so much attention. Probably nothing, she decided. *He's just being nice.*

"Hi, Katarina. I'm Susan, Kevin's sister. It was so hectic at the wedding, I don't think we were ever formally introduced."

"Hello again." Katarina noted the tactful way Susan avoided mentioning her embarrassing fall. Maybe it could be put behind them after all.

"My brother tells me you're a doll maker. I'm guessing it's an incredible coincidence that you are the Kat in Kat's Kreations, right?"

"As a matter of fact, I am. You know my work?"

"I adore them. What else do you design?"

"Porcelain dolls mainly, but I hope to sell the design to some toy manufacturers to make a children's version."

Susan smiled. "I'm sure they'll snatch it up. Kevin says you're also a shrewd businesswoman."

"Thank you. Let's hope so." Katarina felt a peace soothe her nerves. "Right now, I just wish they'd respond. Yes or no—I almost don't even care at this point."

Alex could relate. He'd been there before. Indecision. Apathy. Fear. No use denying the truth. He was there right now. Did he go back to smoke jumping? Or come back to work with Kevin permanently? Or could there be some other reason he felt so unsettled?

He looked at Katarina and felt his emptiness deepen as he recalled her last remark. Flippant didn't fit her style. "That's not true. You've poured your heart into this." She cast him a "how would you know" look, and opened her mouth to protest. "Kevin's told me how much your business means to you."

Her eyebrows shot up in surprise. "Yes, it does. Everything. I merely meant I'm tired of the wait."

"Ah, an impatient woman," he teased.

Katarina crossed her arms in front of her and opened her mouth to retort.

"As well as determined." He had no doubts that Katarina would succeed. She was talented, not to mention as charming as she was beautiful, inside and out. He studied her for a moment, waiting for another objection. The only one he received was her questioning gaze.

"So, Alex. How long are you staying to help Kevin with the business?" his brother-in-law asked. "I thought he only needed temporary help."

He would have preferred to avoid this discussion altogether. "I'm here as long as he needs me. I don't know how long that could take."

"You plan to sit out the fire season?"

He shrugged. "We're taking it one day at a time." He needed to change the subject, and quickly. He didn't want to give Kevin anything more to worry about right now. They had enough to handle without wasting their energy on his problems.

"I thought..."

Alex chuckled. "I need a change of pace." He paused. "Kevin needs me. I won't let him down this time."

Katarina didn't catch on, thankfully, and they seemed to take the hint to drop the subject before she had a chance to ask. The conversation moved on to the others before making the rounds to him again. "So, Adam, Alex, how long is it going to take you two to follow Kevin's example and break this silly agreement you made to avoid marriage?" Susan asked. Though playfully asked, Alex knew the question was totally serious.

Thankfully, Adam beat him to the punch. "Forever. Right, Alex?" The youngest MacIntyre stretched out his hand.

Alex forced a smile and silently agreed, shaking hands with his brother. *Easy for him to say—he has ten years on me.*

Both Elizabeth and Susan scolded them for their boyish attitude. "You can't be serious!" Elizabeth added with a tight-lipped smile. Her husband's arm wrapped around her shoulders, and Alex recalled the other reason he and his brother had made the pact in the first place.

Alex couldn't stand to discuss this now. "Liz, don't take it so seriously. Adam and I haven't thought about it in years."

Adam added his own two cents. "Not since Kevin and Emily broke their engagement—and we can all see that had a happy ending. Don't get all riled up about it." Adam backed off, obviously wanting to placate his sisters and mother, though Alex knew in Adam's own mind nothing had changed. "When the good Lord decides it's time, I'll know it," Adam concluded.

Attempting to add some humor to the conversation, their mother added, "Well then, maybe we'd better have this talk with Him. Sure would save us a whole lot of frustration in *our* efforts."

Adam laughed. "Better yet, why don't you leave the matchmaking to Him in the first place, Mom?"

Alex hadn't dared to look at Katarina throughout this conversation. Now that it was over, he noticed the laughter in her eyes, and relaxed. Hopefully she didn't see the tension stretch between siblings.

The conversation changed again, this time focused on the children, and Adam didn't waste any time slipping away.

Alex was relieved when the chaos subsided and Katarina insisted it was time to get Ricky home and into bed. She turned away, and he noticed something in her ear. He looked again.

It couldn't be. I thought she was joking. He felt like a total fool.

"Katarina." He looked around and realized he didn't want to bring her hearing impairment up in front of everyone and embarrass her further. "Let me walk you and Ricky to your car."

Once they were out of earshot, he gathered his courage. "You must think I'm a real heel."

Katarina looked puzzled. "Now, why would I think such a ridiculous thing?"

"I—I didn't realize," he stammered. "You...I asked if you're deaf. I didn't know."

She tipped her head, concealing her right ear. "Oh. That."

"That." He paused, hoping she would elaborate. She didn't. "I'm sorry."

Ricky reached the car and climbed in. After Katarina buckled his seat belt, she closed the door and turned to Alex. "I didn't take any offense to the comment. It's my own fault. The hearing aid is such a bother in large gatherings."

The silence stretched uncomfortably between them as Katarina walked around the car and opened her door, then started to get inside. He hurried toward her before she could get into the car and leave.

"What about pizza tomorrow night? I don't want to break my promise to Ricky."

Looking up as he approached, Katarina studied him openly. "Ah yes, and it appears you *never* break your promises, right?" Her mouth turned up at the corners. "I plan to catch every word of *this* story."

Alex's heart skipped a beat at her blatant teasing. "There's nothing more to tell. Adam and I agreed long ago that we don't want to be caught."

"I didn't mean to imply anything. Just sounds like a story that needs to be told...one day." She slipped into the car and started the engine.

Alex stared after her until the car's taillights disappeared in the distance.

How long had it been since he'd had dinner with a woman? Never mind that she was engaged, and way too young for him. *This isn't a date,* he reassured himself.

No matter how many times he repeated the sentence, something inside told him otherwise. He recalled Kevin's final advice. "May as well give in now."

Not on your life, Kevin. No bouquet's going to determine my future.

Chapter Five

Katarina scanned the want ads for an apartment where she'd have room to live, make dolls and still manage to save enough money to expand her fledgling company. The designing was going really well, yet she needed to get settled and hire help to keep up with the demands of Kat's Kreations.

She recalled Ron's long-term plans and tried to ignore the shiver that went up her spine. "You need to sell your designs to a company that can put your name all over the world. Let them do the production," he'd insisted, followed by, "Dream big if you're going to dream at all."

Yes, she wanted her business to be successful, but he made it sound so...cold. These were more than dolls—they were her heart and soul. More than simply business. Surely once they married and he trans-

ferred to a Colorado branch, he'd see that. Even
Alex seemed to understand, and he hardly knew her.

Katarina turned back to the baby doll she'd been
dressing before she'd started searching the want ads
for an apartment. She adjusted soft ruffles on the
velveteen skirt, ran her finger over the delicate porcelain nose and gazed into the baby doll's soft
brown eyes.

This is what she truly loved, making something
that would bring a smile to someone's face the same
way each doll did her own. She couldn't deny there
was a certain amount of excitement in the idea of
seeing her own creations in stores across the country. Selling her designs surely didn't mean she'd
have to stop making them, too. And thanks to Alex's
comments yesterday, hope had blossomed within her
again. She dreamed of the day when a children's
version of Kat's Kreations collectable dolls would
be available in toy stores throughout the country.

Ricky and his friends burst into the kitchen, mud
caked on their knees. "Can we have a drink, Auntie
Kat?"

"Sure, go wash your hands." She circled an ad,
then pushed the newspaper aside and poured three
glasses of cherry juice for the boys. The clock above
the fireplace chimed three. "Another hour. What do
you say we go to the park before I take Jacob and
Chad home?"

They cheered. She gathered the boys, loaded them
into the huge plastic wagon and pulled them down

the block. Even after an hour of swinging, sliding and playing space station on the monkey bars, the boys complained when it was time to leave.

"I want a ride in the wagon," Ricky whined.

Ricky had been a handful all day. When she awoke, he'd already tried to fix himself a bowl of cereal for breakfast and spilled milk all over the floor in the process. While cleaning it up, she'd heard a crash upstairs, and had found him exploring the top of his closet.

"Uncle Alex is coming for pizza tonight, isn't he?"

Katarina's heart beat a little faster. She mumbled a confirmation. Her cheeks warmed. Alex MacIntyre was the last person she wanted to see today. He reminded her of a fantasy no man could ever live up to. Mr. Right was an illusion. Reality had burst her hopes of ever finding such a trustworthy man. Over and over again throughout the past twenty years of her life she'd learned that opening her heart only led to pain. First her father, then her fiancé. Stable and predictable didn't look so bad after all.

Why did I have to promise Ricky he could see Alex again today?

Kevin and Emily would be home tomorrow, and Katarina had yet to find a place to live. Emily would try to talk her out of moving, but she realized newlyweds didn't need a houseguest. A new family required time to bond.

Besides, Katarina longed for her own independence, as well. Katarina wanted the freedom to come and go as she pleased. And with her business, she needed room to spread out without imposing on anyone else. She certainly didn't need to worry about who could be getting into it.

When she'd agreed to stay at Emily's house, neither Kevin nor Ricky were a part of Emily's life. Not that Katarina disagreed with their decision to have a quick wedding. That wasn't the case at all. In fact, it was the best solution for everyone.

Even from the beginning, Katarina had never meant to stay more than a few weeks, until she could find a small place of her own.

Kat turned into the driveway, surprised to see Alex waiting on the porch with a pizza box.

"Looks like you wore him out," Alex said, smiling.

She grinned. Ricky was sprawled across the wagon. One leg was tucked into the wagon, the other dangled over the edge. "You mean *finally* wore him out." She parked the wagon and reached for Ricky.

"Here, you take the pizza and open the door. I'll carry him."

Before she had a chance to argue, Katarina had accepted the box and Alex lifted Ricky into his arms. "Where do you want me to lay him?"

Annoyed at how easily she'd let Alex take charge again, she unlocked the front door and pointed to the sofa. "I doubt he'll sleep long."

Katarina continued into the dining room, still upset with herself for not being more assertive. How could she make it clear to Alex MacIntyre that she wasn't some helpless female who needed a man to take care of her? *I have a hearing impairment. I'm not disabled.* Katarina shoved the newspaper to one end of the table and dropped the pizza in the middle, then went to get dishes.

"Ricky's settled. Can I help?"

Katarina spun around. "Do I look like I can't do anything on my own?"

He looked at her as if she'd thrown darts at him. "What in tarnation brought that on?"

She placed her hand upon her hip and looked into his blue eyes, temporarily forgetting what she was going to say. *Good-looking or not, he can't jump in and take over.* "You do...um, did...uh, every time I see you, you assume I can't handle anything."

"I what?" His blue eyes widened. "How do I do that?"

Katarina crossed her arms over her beating heart, raised one arm and rested her finger on her chin. "Hmm, let's see now. You yanked me out from under the table...."

"You were stuck. I was trying to help," he protested.

"I would have been absolutely content to stay out of the limelight after that humiliation, thank you very much. Then you insisted on carrying those flower vases to my car. You charged right in to get Ricky out of the tree...."

Alex clenched his jaw and his face turned red. "And what would you have liked me to do? Stand there and give you a list of my qualifications to rescue a frightened little boy? Or were you thinking you'd climb the tree in that frilly dress of yours?"

"That isn't the point. However, you could have explained instead of rushing right in and taking charge. Which brings us to today. I'm perfectly capable of carrying Ricky inside. And now you assume I need your help in the kitchen." She stepped around the counter and reached up to open the cabinet. "I do believe I'm..."

Alex put his hand against the cabinet door to hold it closed. Surprised, she looked over her shoulder, inhaling his clean outdoorsy scent. Her gaze moved from his long, muscled arm to his shoulder, neck and finally to his freshly shaven jaw. *He didn't come straight from work. He took the time to go home and shower.*

"I happen to love kids, okay? I've already lost too much time with my sisters' children. I don't plan to miss the chance to spend time with Ricky. And as far as my offer to help, I'm not one of those chauvinistic men who thinks a woman's place is in the kitchen. I was raised sharing the load. You have a problem with any of that?" Alex's clipped words forbade questioning him further.

Alex's explanation took the punch from Kat's anger. She'd fought for everything as a young child, constantly fended off illness and struggled to keep up with missed schoolwork. Maybe that was why she was so determined to be independent. *What's wrong with me?* She felt Alex's nearness, confused by the quickening of her heart and shortness of breath. Somehow, a smile found its way through the mask of uncertainty. "No problem. Just so we understand each other."

Alex bent his elbow and leaned closer. His gaze caressed her face before he offered a forgiving smile. "Who is it that doesn't understand your capabilities, Katarina? Because it certainly isn't me. I wouldn't dream of standing in your way."

She looked at his feet, then into his eyes. "Talk's cheap."

His smile disappeared and he backed across the kitchen. With one of Alex's hands resting upon the counter and the thumb of his other hand hooked in his jeans pocket, his shoulders looked even broader than they had up close.

Katarina turned her back to him, opened the cabinet and closed her eyes, hoping to catch her breath and recollect the protective wit that served as her shield of armor. Not even Ron could unravel her as Alex had after only two days.

"So, is there anything I may do to help, or would you prefer I go sit down?"

"I'll have everything together in just a minute."

Alex moved to the dining-room side of the island

dividing the two rooms. He didn't much like the image Katarina seemed to have of him. Though he heard her reasons, he still didn't understand what he'd done wrong. Was it so terrible to be helpful? To be a considerate guest? He knew the logical answers to the questions, but couldn't for the life of him figure out why the obvious wasn't clear to Katarina. "May I ask you a question?"

"Sure," Katarina said, cheerful again. She brought in the plates and glasses, then returned to the kitchen and opened the refrigerator.

He hemmed and hawed for a minute, still uncertain if it was wise to push her. "Could you help me understand exactly how to correct my mistakes…um, so I don't make the same ones with anyone else?"

"Anyone else?" Katarina pulled out a cutting board and placed it on the counter between them. "I thought you weren't interested in being 'caught.'" She raised her eyebrows and shot him a devastatingly beautiful grin as she chopped up a head of lettuce.

"Who said anything about anyone catching me?"

She scooped up a handful of lettuce and placed it into a bowl. "Ah, you're just in it for the chase, huh?"

He shook his head and leaned across the counter. "Never said that, either. I just don't like walking on burning embers. I have enough of that in my line of work."

Katarina stifled a laugh, picking up each stray piece of lettuce. "I'm sorry for snapping at you."

"I wasn't asking for an apology." He covered her hands with his own and waited for her reply. There was none. "Why did that offend you so, offering to help?"

"Are you always so pushy?"

He smiled. "Yeah, I guess I am. Is that what's bothering you? You don't like people to ask too many questions? Or don't you want to let anyone get too close?"

She paused, staring him in the eye with a cool smile on her lips. "I simply don't 'need' people the way a lot of other women do."

"Fiercely independent," he said, assessing her. "You don't want to be depended upon, or to depend on anyone else?"

Silence.

"Guess I hit a nerve."

"Are you a psychologist in the off-season?" Katarina pulled her hands loose and opened a brown paper sack in front of her. "Hmm, a smoke jumping shrink. Has a nice ring to it."

Alex chuckled.

She took out two Italian tomatoes, washed them, quartered them and tossed them into the salad.

"So, you think accepting help is a sign of weakness?"

"Listen, Doc…"

"That's your sister. My crew calls me Mac, but

I really prefer it if you'd stick to Alex. Bury the hatchet, Katarina. You don't need anyone, and I'm not in the market to be needed. You're as good as engaged—'' he cocked his head ''—though I don't quite understand why you're here, and he's not.''

She smiled. ''Ron happens to believe in individual independence. He encourages it, in fact. He doesn't want me to depend upon him any more than I want to.''

''Probably believes in prenuptial contracts, too,'' Alex muttered.

''And what's wrong with that?''

He'd better stop before they were at each other's throats again, he thought. What in the world had given her such a distorted view? All he'd done was offer a little help.

''Alex? Why don't you approve of prenuptial agreements?''

His name rolled off her tongue like a breeze through the forest—soft, gentle and refreshing. ''Never mind. Just a different view of commitment, I guess. But what do I know? I'm thirty-five and haven't even been close to the altar. You on the other hand…are as good as engaged. Friends?''

Her mouth twisted into a crooked grin. ''On the other hand, I'm no expert, either. This will be my second engagement, and I'm not so convinced it's a great idea, either.'' She extended her hand. ''Friends.''

Alex took her graceful hand into his and met her

coy smile with one of his own. "Which aren't you sure of, Katarina? The prenuptial agreement or the engagement?"

Katarina thought for a moment.

"Neither."

Chapter Six

Katarina looked out the window. "What is Alex doing here again?" Emily and Kevin had returned from their honeymoon less than an hour ago.

Kevin moved their suitcases out of the way. "I called him on the way into town. He needs some invoices signed. What do you mean, 'again'?" Before Kat could answer, the doorbell rang, and Kevin rushed through the house to answer it, Ricky right on his heels.

Not ready to face another hundred and one questions from the smoke jumping shrink, Katarina suggested she and Emily take their tea to the deck in the backyard.

"Bearly Toys just called, and want to see my designs and a prototype," she said when they were settled.

"Katarina!" Emily gasped. "That's wonderful. When is the presentation?"

Katarina took a deep breath and mentally slowed her racing mind. "Wednesday. At eleven. They're trying to beat a deadline. That's why I have to get on the road as soon as possible. It's around a thousand miles. I figure it should take—"

"What? That's the day after tomorrow." Emily furrowed her eyebrows. "You're going to drive a thousand miles? Why don't you fly?"

Katarina stood up and walked over to the deck railing. "Right, I'm going to get my entire portfolio into two suitcases. And even if I could, do you know how much airfare is to Spokane?"

"Spokane? Kat..." Emily started to protest.

"I can't afford to fly. End of discussion. According to the map site on the Internet, I'll make it in plenty of time." Katarina had been suppressing a scream of excitement since the call had come early that morning, and now finally let out a high-pitched squeal. She'd called Ron to share her news, but he'd had to rush off to a meeting.

"Congratulations, Katarina." Alex's voice resounded through the house and out the screen door. He slid the screen open and the two men joined them. Ricky rushed past them to climb on his new swing set. "I didn't mean to eavesdrop, but I could hardly miss the news. Would you mind giving me a lift?"

He casually wrapped an arm around her shoulder

and gave her a friendly hug. Katarina tried to ignore the piney scent of Alex's aftershave. "Thanks, but where are you needing to go? I'm going to Washington." Katarina stepped away.

"I'm aware of where Spokane is. Missoula is right on the way. If Kevin's going to need me to help him for a while longer, I need my own truck." Alex leaned back against the deck railing and crossed his arms over his chest. "I can't keep borrowing everything, especially now that we aren't in the same house. I'd be glad to share the driving and the expenses. As you say, airfare isn't cheap. You'd save me a lot of money, and having a second driver would make the trip easier."

Kevin had a puzzled smile on his face.

"That's a perfect solution!" Emily got out of her chair and nuzzled up to her husband. "Isn't it, Kevin?"

"That's great news, Katarina. Sounds like Alex has everything at work running smoothly and we're back on schedule. It would be a big help to have his own supplies. I don't see any problem with you going, Alex."

Katarina was speechless. She looked from Emily to Kevin to Alex.

"I'm so relieved you won't be driving alone," Emily exclaimed.

Kevin agreed.

Alex waited for her response.

There was no way Katarina could explain why

this was a terrible idea without her sister claiming Katarina still had that teenage crush on the man. There couldn't be anything further from the truth. Having had three days to get to know him better, she knew her first impression of Alex was obviously wrong. *Mr. Nice Guy—what a joke.* The man was annoying. He was domineering, pushy and presumptuous. That might work on a mountainside, but not on her!

Yet, before she knew it, Alex had convinced her to let him ride all the way to Montana with her. He and Kevin left, while she and Emily packed.

Katarina added the finishing touches to her portfolio of drawings and tried to make her sister understand why she wanted to find a place of her own. Then Katarina, Emily and Ricky had the oil changed on the car and filled it with gas. On the way home, Katarina took Emily to see the apartment she had looked at to rent. When they returned to Emily's, the discussion was still going strong.

"You don't even know how long you're going to need a place to live, Katarina. And if you do get married, what if Ron doesn't want to move to Colorado after all? What if you sell your designs to a company that wants you to relocate? Kevin and I don't mind if you stay here until you're more certain of your plans."

"I came here to set up my business, Emily. Ron understands how important this is to me."

Emily sighed. "How many times have you two broken up in the two years you've dated, Kat?"

"This isn't the same. We're just taking a short break to concentrate on our careers before we have to settle down."

"If the man were any more settled, he'd be petrified, Kat. Surely you don't think that's going to change? I cannot see you 'settled down' with anyone, let alone Ron. If he wanted to be here with you, he would be."

"We have complementing personalities," called Katarina as she carried the last ten-gallon tote from the basement to the back of her station wagon. She hoped her sister would stop talking about Ron before Alex returned.

When she saw Alex at the top of the stairs, Katarina realized it was already too late. He'd probably heard the entire argument. Without a word, Alex stepped out of her way.

"Wise move," Emily quipped from behind her.

Katarina watched Alex stuff his backpack and sleeping bag into her car.

"A sleeping bag? I certainly hope you don't think *I'm* camping out. We're stopping at a hotel." How she'd ever been convinced to go along with this, she'd never know. She must have lost her mind.

"Call it my security blanket, then. I don't drive anywhere without one." He carefully set her bag on top.

Katarina tried to ignore the way his lip quirked

up on one side. The man was too charming. That was it. He'd caught her in a weak moment of exhilaration.

I'm pathetic. Where's my spine? What in the world will I find to talk to him about? Nothing, if she was smart. She'd keep her mouth shut before she made a further fool of herself. It seemed every time they were together, she put her foot in her mouth.

Katarina jumped when the smooth timbre of Alex's voice interrupted her thoughts. "That's all I have. Do you have anything else to load?" They hadn't even pulled out of the driveway yet, and his voice was already irritatingly familiar.

She hoped he hadn't noticed her staring at him. "No, that's everything." She turned to Emily and forced a smile. "I'll see you by the end of the week, sis. And remember, if Mrs. Simmons calls about that apartment, I want it."

"You don't want that tiny place, Kat. We'll come up with something better." Emily's smile was full of mischief. What did she have up her sleeve now? Katarina shook her head. There was no use arguing.

"Oh, if Ron calls, tell him I'll call him from the hotel tonight. Bye-bye, Ricky. You be a good boy." Katarina gave him a hug, knowing she would miss him more than she wanted to admit. After only three weeks together, she'd kind of gotten used to his boisterous energy, almost as if they were kindred spirits.

Emily and Ricky stood on the porch hand in hand. "Have a nice trip, *you two*."

Katarina glanced at Alex, then glared at her sister. *I hope he didn't notice the teasing lilt to Emily's voice.*

No way were Katarina and Alex going to find common ground. She was only doing him a favor. After two days she'd be free of him and his annoying charm. With any luck, he'd return to jumping into fires, and she'd have an all-new plan for her business.

Katarina had spent the past week pondering her sisters' accusations that she wouldn't marry Ron. What made Emily and Lisa so sure? Just because Katarina had momentarily forgotten his name at the wedding, it didn't mean she didn't take the relationship seriously. She and Ron had dated for almost two years. He was trustworthy, understanding and nice-looking. Who wanted a guy so handsome that all the women would be chasing him?

She buckled her seat belt and turned the key in the ignition, stealing a glance at Alex. It wasn't his fault that he was too attractive, too charming and too close for comfort.

Help me to be civil to him, Lord. And help these two days pass quickly. She realized there must be a reason Alex made her so uncomfortable. *God, why do You keep bringing Alex into my life? I'm going to marry Ron. I've been down the road of failure*

*with one attractive older man— I'm not interested
in trying it again.*

Alex tucked his long legs into the passenger seat
and his knees nearly touched the dash, yet he remained silent. She waited a few minutes to see if
he'd say or do anything. He didn't.

"You can move the seat back if you'd like. It's
a split bench," she said, trying to tame her irritation.

"I'll be okay. Besides, it can't go back any farther. You have supplies behind the seat."

Katarina shifted to Park and looked at him. "So
you were going to ride for eight hours like that?"

"I had faith in you." One corner of his mouth
turned up. The twinkle in his blue eyes told her that
he would have spent the next nine hundred miles
like this just waiting for her to prove his point.

She didn't need him flirting with her. It was going
to be difficult enough spending the next two days
together without any other complications. Ron had
been happy to learn that she'd have Kevin's big
brother along to help drive. He wouldn't be if he
saw the man.

Was that why she was so edgy? Because she'd
been too chicken to tell her almost-fiancé that Alex
was single, and six feet six inches of rugged mas-
culinity? Because she found Alex MacIntyre not
only physically attractive, but intellectually, as well?
Or because she was terrified to think that her sisters
were right, that Ron wasn't the right man for her?

I'm going to marry Ron. I am. Why is everyone trying to confuse me?

Ron might not be all that her first fiancé hadn't been, but he wasn't exactly chopped liver, either. They knew everything about each other. There would be no surprises with Ron. Eight weeks from now, he would propose. Two years later, they'd start a family. It was part of the plan, and Ron planned everything down to the tiniest detail. He probably had the exact time he would propose written into his computer day planner. Stable and predictable. That was what she needed from a man, wasn't it?

Katarina crawled out of the car and walked around to the passenger side. She opened the back door and yanked the tall basket from the floor behind the seat, rearranged the plastic totes and set the basket on top. "Go ahead and move the seat. It should even recline, if you want."

She stepped back. When she turned, he was standing beside her, towering above her by nearly eight inches. "Thanks."

Katarina tipped her chin up, and up. "I can't believe you were waiting for me to say something. It could have been hours before I realized."

"But it wasn't."

She put her hands on her hips and pressed her face closer to his. "But it could have been."

His smile broadened. "And I must say, I'm flattered that you noticed."

Katarina jerked back. "Well, you shouldn't be."

She slammed the door closed and walked back to the driver's seat.

Emily laughed. "Hey, you two, I'm expecting a complete family gathering this Christmas. And I don't want either of you to ruin my plans! Now, quit behaving like a couple of twelve-year-olds."

Alex laughed. "I'm sure we'll find plenty to talk about."

"Then you must like talking to yourself," Katarina grumbled as she got in and turned the key, grinding the already revving ignition.

"I'll see you soon, buddy," Alex said to Ricky.

He beamed, then gave Alex a "super-duper" bear hug.

Alex stepped over to Emily and gave her a hug. "You make sure that brother of mine takes it easy."

"And you take care of my sister, would you?"

"My pleasure."

Katarina beeped the horn. "We don't have all night."

Alex crawled into the car and clicked his seat belt. "I wouldn't bet on that."

Chapter Seven

Katarina was doing a fine job of pretending Alex wasn't there. If they were going to spend the next nine hundred miles together, he thought, they could at least get to know a little about each other, couldn't they? It didn't mean he needed her, or she needed him. Didn't have to mean that, anyway.

At first he'd thought she was simply preoccupied with driving through the heavy summer traffic. Businessmen flew down the highway as if they were headed to a fire. Add to that the first of the summer tourists, motor homes, and it was a full-fledged mess.

Katarina turned on the radio and set her cruise control, allowing those in a hurry to buzz on past.

"So, tell me about your business. How'd you ever get started making dolls?" Alex asked half an hour later, after deciding she wasn't going to initiate conversation.

"I'm sure the last thing you want to know about is my dolls." She ran her hand through her short hair and tucked a strand behind her ear, then pulled it out again.

"Why are you so determined we can't be friends?"

She remained silent.

Without her hair pulled back, Alex could barely see the hearing aid. He wondered if she'd turned it off again, and spoke a little louder. "I know I stuck my foot in my mouth right off the bat, and I can't apologize enough."

"You don't have to yell—it's on." Her eyes didn't leave the highway. "I asked you to forget that. I don't want your pity."

"I'm not offering any, so don't make me give it." He rubbed the pain in his knee. "We're going to be in this car for close to sixteen hours. There's no reason we can't talk, is there?" *She's wearing that perfume again.*

She glanced at him, then back to the road. "I can't believe you want to talk about dolls. Doesn't seem like you. Now, if you'd asked about my hearing, that would seem more like a guy."

So that was the barricade. He smiled, shaking his head, hoping to reassure her he wasn't trying to pry. "I don't want to hear anything you don't want to tell me. If and when you do, I'll listen. Until then,

I'm certain there's something we can discuss. And for the record, dolls don't scare me, either.'' He turned slightly to face her, then rested his arm on the back of the seat. She didn't jump as she had on the porch swing in the gazebo. That in itself was a relief. "From what my sisters tell me, I take it these dolls of yours aren't the average wet-and-cry babies I see on the shelves every Christmas.''

The beginning of a smile teased the corner of her mouth, allowing her true personality to peek through. "No, not yet, anyway. Right now I only sell porcelain dolls, design their clothing and make a few stuffed animals called Kat's Kritters. But I'd love nothing more than to see children enjoy actually playing with a Kat's Kreation. Hopefully Bearly Toys will like the idea as well as I do.''

He listened as she went on about the selection process and what Katarina hoped it would mean for her company.

The mood lightened considerably as Kat's passion for her creations overflowed like bubbles from a root beer float.

Her enthusiasm took him back to the days when he'd been young and full of dreams. How long had it been since he'd felt for his job what she did for hers? He didn't want to think about it. Especially not right now. He'd much rather share Katarina's excitement than try to find his own again.

"Susan and Liz went on for an hour about your dolls after you left the other night.'' He motioned over his shoulder with his thumb. "So all this stuff back here is what you turn into your classic creations, huh?"

Katarina gasped and her hand flew to her chest. "Stuff? That 'stuff' is my livelihood," she wailed dramatically as she broke into an irresistibly devastating smile that didn't begin to disguise the serious scolding she was giving him. "I don't go anywhere without it. You can't call it 'stuff' until you've at least carried it up three flights of stairs. And back down again."

He laughed softly. "I stand corrected. I guess I better make sure I qualify by the end of this trip then, hadn't I?" Alex tore his gaze from her, suddenly uncomfortable being in such tight quarters with Katarina. What was it about her that tugged at him? Maybe getting to know her wasn't such a great idea after all. In a few weeks he'd be off to some remote forest fire.

He studied the sparsely covered bluffs and pointed out the herd of antelope who were hoping for a meal.

Katarina quickly glanced at them. "There are so many of them. It's hard to believe there's going to be enough grass for everyone, isn't it?"

"God provides what they need."

Her only reply was a soft "Hmmm."

They crossed the Wyoming border, and immediately ran into road construction. Katarina pulled to a stop behind the long row of cars. "How long do

you suppose this will take?'' Though the car ahead
of her hadn't moved at all, she continually eased her
sandaled foot from the brake as if it would make the
traffic move.

She was getting pretty close to the car ahead of
them, and he found himself pressing against the
floorboard. ''Who knows how long it'll take? You
may as well put it in Park and shut off the air con-
ditioner so the engine doesn't overheat.''

There was a long hesitation before she followed
his suggestion. Within a few minutes it got stuffy
inside, and she opened the windows, then leaned
out. She looked forward, then behind. ''I can't even
see any highway department vehicles. What's going
on?''

''It is the season for construction. Good thing you
don't have that interview tomorrow.''

The smile on her lips wavered a bit. ''What's one
delay going to mean, another half hour? No big deal,
right?''

''Right.'' He didn't want to point out that where
there was one highway under construction, there
were probably five more. She was hopeful, and so
was he—hopeful that her optimism paid off.

Half an hour later they'd finally passed through
Cheyenne, ready to make up the time they'd lost.
Less than sixty miles later, the dreaded orange signs
appeared again. As they approached the flagman, he
stepped closer to the center line and waved the stop

sign. The man leaned toward the car and Katarina opened the window.

"It's going to be a forty-five-minute wait."

Katarina groaned and turned the car off.

Alex shrugged, got out to stretch and wound up visiting with the highway crew for most of the delay. He leaned his hand on Katarina's window. "There's major work on the interstate all the way to Bozeman. At least four more long delays that they're aware of."

"You're kidding." The locket clung to Katarina's moist skin ninety degrees off-kilter. She folded a tiny doll dress, put it into the basket and replaced the lid, then pulled a small sketch pad from the door pocket and began to fan herself. "What a bother."

"We could cut across the state," he suggested. *I wonder if her fiancé's picture is inside the locket. She wears it most of the time.*

"But we can make up a little time in between construction zones if we stay on the interstate."

"Okay. It's up to you." He walked around to the other side and crawled back into the car. The flagman spun the sign to slow, and waved her forward.

The hazed, dingy, mud-color sky seemed to drown out the sun. Dust devils blew dirt across the road, pelting the car with sand. Clouds of bugs were thick. It was unbearably hot, with not even a thundercloud in sight.

The pop radio station faded as they disappeared into the valley. Katarina hit the scan button in search of another. The blue iridescent numbers scrolled past, and back around to where they'd started. She switched to another band, finding only small stations with a sad array of music or livestock reports. "I can't believe I forgot to bring my music."

She pulled off at the first exit and began to look for a restaurant. The two local diners were closed, so they filled the car with gas and grabbed some snacks to hold them over till they reached Casper. Alex joined Katarina at the register with his arms full. She looked at him, then at the water, two juices and two sodas in his arms. He looked into her eyes. "Just in case."

She splayed her hand on her hip. "In case what? I don't do 'just in cases.'"

He smiled in spite of her naiveté. "Good, you're welcome to say 'I told you so' when we arrive at my place with two full bottles of unused water."

She smiled at his challenge. "I'll do that."

"I didn't know which you'd prefer to drink, so I got a little of everything."

She simply stared at him and her eyes misted over, then she spun around and was out the door. He handed the clerk a twenty-dollar bill and pocketed his change, not even waiting for a bag to carry everything in. He followed her outside. "Katarina! What did I do wrong this time?"

Katarina Berthoff was nothing like the women he met in his line of work. Not that he had any complaints about them, per se. But there was something very different about a soot-covered woman carrying a hundred-pound pack on her back and the equally determined, yet undeniably feminine creature walking in front of him. Watching her, he decided it was no wonder his mind had gone up in smoke the day his brother married her sister.

Her yellow-and-white-knit sundress fit as if it were made specially for her. Was it the shade of yellow, or the wonderful way her face glowed? Rows of white leather flowers covered the straps of her sandals, showing off her pretty pink toenails. Sunshine. No other way to describe her, he decided.

Katarina got into the station wagon, closed the door and started the engine. Trying to hurry, Alex hit his head ducking into the seat beside her. He dropped the drinks at his feet, closed the door and took hold of her hand before she could shift into gear.

"Hold on right there!"

Tears trickled down her cheeks.

"Kat," he whispered. He let go of her hand, placed his fingertips on her chin and gently turned her to face him. "What did I say?"

"I told you before, Alex, I don't need you. I didn't need you to come along to take care of me." She gasped for air. "I don't need you to tell me how to drive, or see that I have something to drink." She carried on, her voice and temper escalating. *She's about to hyperventilate.*

"Cool down, Katarina. You're taking this a bit

too far.'' He opened the bottle of cold water and offered her a drink. ''Kat, come on, take a sip of water.''

She pushed it away. He felt it slipping from his hand and clutched it tighter, spraying her with the icy-cold liquid. Her eyes shot open and she gasped.

He stared at her, wide-eyed. ''I didn't mean to do that!''

She took two deep breaths, then another one. ''I've managed on my own all these years, Alex. I don't need or want a father to take care of me now.''

He slammed his palm on the top of the water spout. *A father? She thinks I'm trying to replace her...father?* Feeling as if he'd just been doused in cold water himself, he leaned his head back. ''You don't have to worry, Katarina.'' He closed his eyes and took a deep breath, trying to understand what was happening between them. ''The *last* thing I want to be is a father figure to you.''

Just hearing those words made everything crystal clear. Though he hadn't given it too much thought, he had to admit, he hadn't totally ruled out a relationship with Katarina. Reason had told him that she was his little sister's age, and he had quickly dispelled the comparison. But her *father?* It was a bit much.

No use hoping there could ever be something between them. They were at two opposite stages in their lives. She was young and energetic, ready to experience life to its fullest. He, on the other hand, had seen the best the world had to offer and longed to settle down, find someone to share his life, maybe even start a family.

Her father? He groaned silently.

Katarina pulled onto the highway without another word.

He needed a distraction. Why hadn't he thought to look on the rack for the latest John Grisham novel? "If you'd like me to drive, just let me know. Otherwise, I'll try not to bother you."

Alex wiped sweat from his brow and instantly remembered the friends and responsibilities he'd left behind. They were probably off to a fire somewhere by now.

His mind was no longer on the lovely woman next to him, but stuck on the current drought. As much as he tried to forget, the career he'd put on hold haunted him. There was no way he could douse the guilt that gnawed at his gut. His mother's call to help Kevin had come right before the doctor's appointment that would have cleared him to return to fighting fires.

Why did he try to kid himself? He knew his leg was ready, but he was far from it. Despite the accident, jumping out of a DC-3 didn't bother him, but what would be waiting for him when he hit the ground did. He tried to forget memories of the two friends who wouldn't be with him this year. He should have been there that day. Why had his best friend failed to see the severity of the fire, leaving a young widow and baby behind?

Fires were unpredictable by nature. That was one of the first concepts he'd learned. Yet it hadn't stopped him from jumping into the middle of a blazing forest for the past eight years. Now, suddenly, it seemed unimportant. He knew better, but for some reason, it just wasn't enough.

Kevin had mentioned needing help running his expanding company. They had tried it once before. And he'd been the one to walk away, leaving Kevin to find his own way. Alex had wanted adventure, and if the truth be known, he didn't care about the element of danger the job involved.

He glanced at Katarina. *What are you trying to tell me, God? Just when I think I know the plan, I hit a smoke screen.*

And the current smoke screen had a name. Sweet, optimistic-to-a-fault, yet deeply hurting…Katarina.

Alex recalled the day he and Adam had made that ridiculously childish pact. In eight years he hadn't been as tempted to break it as he had in the past four days.

This is ludicrous, he thought. *There's no such thing as love at first sight.*

Chapter Eight

Katarina closed her window and fanned herself with her pocket calendar at the third construction zone. What should have been a five-hour drive had taken nearly seven, and they weren't even close to Montana yet. She started the engine and turned the fan to high.

"What are you doing?"

He watched her turn the vents toward her.

"What does it look like? I can't stand this dusty hot air any longer. Just a few minutes." He started to repeat his warning about the car overheating when she lifted her finger to her mouth to shush him. "If we hit one more construction zone, I'm going to scream."

Alex didn't say another word.

Not even when it took another ten minutes for traffic to move through the road construction. Not even when the temperature warning light came on. Not even when it meant sitting in the unbearable heat for an hour before Alex could go near the radiator. They'd barely pulled into the restaurant in Casper before the temperature gauge began rising again. By mutual consent they agreed to look for a place to stay for the night. They called all the motels listed in the phone directory, disappointed to find no vacancies for a hundred miles.

She was exhausted. "I wish we could get out of this heat."

"Be careful what you ask for—you just might get it."

Before leaving town, they stopped for gasoline. Katarina started filling the tank with fuel and Alex opened the hood.

"What's wrong now?"

"I want to check all the fluid levels." A few minutes later, he headed into the convenience store.

Katarina scrubbed the bugs from the windshield while she waited. In addition to paying for the gas, Alex emerged with another gallon of water, engine coolant, oil, windshield washer fluid and a small Styrofoam cooler.

"What's that? Heavens, we just ate half the restaurant. And I had the oil changed before we left."

"Then I wouldn't bother going back to the same place again. I'm afraid they took you, big time. Either that, or your car goes through fluids faster than I do," he grumbled. "I hope this takes care of everything. I bought a couple of sandwiches in case we need a snack." Alex set the cooler in the back seat. "The clerk confirmed that construction report. He suggested we cut across through Yellowstone. What do you think? There shouldn't be any traffic this time of night." He proceeded to add the oil and fill the radiator as they talked.

Katarina rested her hip against the car and crossed her arms. "It sounds so isolated, but I can't take another delay, either. I'll do whatever you think is best."

Alex touched her forehead with the back of his hand. "You aren't feverish. Maybe it's heat exhaustion."

She gave him a playful pout.

"So, what's up?" He closed the hood, then smiled.

She looked at him again, this time less upset that she'd let him come. If she'd been alone, she'd still be stuck on the interstate, waiting in an endless line of traffic. "I think it's your turn to drive. I haven't a clue where we're going."

"Aha, I knew the other shoe was about to fall." He looked at his watch. "Even if we stop to rest somewhere along the way, we should make it to my place by tomorrow evening, and you'll have another day to get to Spokane. Might even have a chance to show off the sights. You ever been to Yellowstone?"

"No." She had to admit, the scenery part sounded

nice. She'd had it with traffic jams, exhaust, heat and the dry, dusty, barren plains.

"You're sure you're not going to change your mind? I realize it is a woman's prerogative. I don't want to take over or anything."

She crawled into the passenger seat and clicked her seat belt for emphasis. "She's all yours. Do you need the map?"

Alex laughed. He pushed the seat back and slipped behind the steering wheel. "Where do you think we are, the Old West? They don't use trees as landmarks anymore."

"Could have fooled me."

A few miles down the road, the teasing lilt of Katarina's voice broke the silence. "So, devoted bachelor, tell me about this pact you and your baby brother have."

"We don't need to go there, Miss Practically Engaged. So what does this mean, anyway? How does one get to be 'practically engaged'?"

Katarina let out a theatrical sigh. "Well, I'm certainly not going to tell you if you're not going to tell me about the pact."

"Fine with me." He turned to look out the window. Alex reached into the back seat and pulled out a cassette. "Hope you don't mind—thought it might beat livestock reports and static." He pushed the tape into the player and adjusted the volume. "There wasn't much to choose from. I at least recognized this name."

Faith Hill began her lively concert. A while later, she noticed Alex rub his leg just above the knee. Being cramped up in the car certainly hadn't been easy on it.

Katarina saw lights ahead. "I think we'd better find someplace to stay the night, Alex. We both need to stretch out and get a good night's sleep."

He rubbed his leg again, then asked her to get him a cold soda from the cooler. He chugged half of it before saying a word. "We're almost to Thermopolis. We can see if there's a couple of rooms there. If not...I have to be honest, the chances of finding anything are slim before we're in the park."

Alex should have warned her that they'd need reservations. Motel rooms were in short supply in this part of the country. He yawned. An hour later, their last hope diminished, he headed north.

It was apparent that if he wanted to bridge that gap between him and Katarina, he was going to have to take the first step. "You going to sleep, or are you willing to take a chance on getting to know one another? I'm afraid we have plenty of time to burn."

Katarina giggled. "Cute."

"It's about time you appreciated my humor. So, what do you say— I'll tell you my story, and you tell me yours. If nothing else, it will help make the trip go faster."

She looked at him skeptically. Finally she agreed. "May as well jump right in. You lead."

Alex turned on his brights and set the cruise control. It felt good to laugh with her. "I think I'll let you win, before I go up in smoke."

"Ooh, you're on fire now."

He groaned. "I think that proves we're exhausted. Adam and I made 'our pact,' as you call it, after Emily broke the engagement. Our dad——"

"Wait just a minute. After Emily broke the engagement? Kevin refused to go with her so she could attend medical school."

"That's not the whole story, but they're together again, remember? There's no use arguing the point now."

"But arguing with you is such fun." She smiled.

He glanced at her in disbelief, keeping one eye on the road. "Is that what this has been all about?"

"What can you say—when you're hot, you're hot."

Alex cleared his throat, hoping to put out the fire that was about to blow up in both of their faces. "Maybe we'd both be better off if you went to sleep."

She giggled. "I'm sorry. Go ahead with your story."

"As I was saying, six months after they broke up, our dad died, we closed down Dad's business, Mom went through a bad spell trying to handle everything, then Liz and her husband lost their six-month-old daughter in a fire. It does things to you, experiencing that much loss in such a short time."

Katarina touched his arm. "I'm sorry, Alex. That must have been very difficult."

Her hand felt like a feather. Soft, delicate and reassuring.

"That's been a long time now." Her voice faltered. "Haven't you ever heard the saying, 'Better to have loved and lost than never to have loved at all'? Don't you want to get married some day?"

"I'll plead the fifth on that last one." He glanced at Katarina, wondering how many men she'd loved and lost. "You actually believe the first one?"

"I guess I do. I wouldn't be thinking of getting married if I didn't." She turned around in the seat to dig for her stitching and turned the map light on. "Does the light bother you?"

"No, it's fine."

From under the seat she brought a box of disposable washcloths and wiped her hands before taking the fabric from the basket. "Until Ron and I do get married, I want to see the country and enjoy myself. There isn't much time before we'll settle down and have children. I don't want to wait until I'm an old maid to start a family, either."

"By all means, you'd better hurry and lasso that boyfriend of yours, then."

"And what is that supposed to mean?"

He was beginning to sound and feel like some jealous old man. "You make it sound like some business merger instead of love."

"We've been dating nearly two years."

"So why aren't you married, then?" he challenged.

Katarina looked at him with those bright blue eyes wide and a defensive smile on her lips. "If you must know, he's going to ask me on August fifteenth, our second anniversary."

"Now, that sounds romantic. Why wait, if you're so much in love? Or are you?"

"Would I date someone for that long and not love him?" she demanded, her voice quivering.

"And two years proves you're in love? You are a dreamer, Katarina." She didn't reply. "I'm sorry, but how long you date has nothing to do with the success of a marriage. I've known couples who have been together for years whose marriages fell apart. And couples who by some miracle know immediately that they're right for one another—who are there for one another through thick and thin, good times and bad. That's love."

"Ron sends me flowers every Friday."

"A real Boy Scout, huh? Sounds like an accountant with an efficient secretary." Alex slowed to round a curve.

"You ought to talk—you won't even commit to a relationship. You'd rather stick to some childish pact with your brother."

He hesitated, assessing her for a moment. "The life of a smokejumper isn't easy on relationships. I haven't committed myself because I refuse to leave a wife to worry and raise the kids alone. If I found someone I'm crazy enough about to marry, I couldn't leave her six months out of the year. When I find her, she's going to be my first priority, not some job.''

There was a long silence. ''Then maybe you should find someone who likes adventure and traveling, and let her go with you. There are plenty of people who take their family with them on a job. Look at actors and singers.''

There was more to it than the traveling, but he couldn't begin to explain that to a dreamer like Katarina. He'd said far more than he should have already. He pressed the accelerator and hoped she'd let the subject die.

''Don't you have some wonderful advice for me?''

He heard a glint of amusement in her voice, saw a hint of a smile on her face. ''Yeah, your fiancé is a fool for letting you out of his sight.''

Katarina couldn't work. She put the doll clothes away and pretended to doze, bewildered by Alex's remarks. Why was he so upset with her? They'd listened to both sides of that tape at least five times. If she heard one more song about a brokenhearted cowboy she'd walk back home. She wondered what in the world kept bringing on the arguments between them. The romantic in her said only one reason made sense. But that was impossible. They'd known each other only a week. Besides, she was practically engaged to someone else. She couldn't be falling in love with Alex.

Katarina tucked her feet up onto the seat and leaned her head against the door. The music faded away and she felt the pressure of the day slip into the comfort of silence....

...Some sixth sense brought her fully awake.

"Hang on!" Alex's hand pressed her against the seat.

The car slid off the road and rolled to its side, to the top, then over again. Her sewing basket hit her in the head. The totes and cooler tumbled in the back end as if they were in a clothes dryer. Finally they came to a sudden stop. A terrible clanging forced him to turn the car off.

"Katarina, you okay?"

"What happened?"

"I swerved to miss a deer and hit a boulder in the road. Are you hurt?" He flicked the lights on.

She shook her head. "I hit my head on something, but I think I'm okay. Are you? Okay, I mean."

"I'm fine. We need to get out of here. Grab your things, quick. Don't forget the cell phone."

The headlights glared into the abyss. Alex opened the back end and pulled everything out. "Move things farther away from the car. Gas is leaking." When they were through, he pointed a flashlight toward the road. "If this is the detour, I'd hate to see what the highway looks like. I've four-wheeled on better."

"There was *more* road construction?"

He nodded.

Katarina headed back to the car, muttering.

"Katarina? Did you forget something?"

He watched in silence as she walked a wide circle and looked at her car. Weeds stuck out from the back doors. The top looked like an accordion, the front end like a mountain range. One headlight was gone.

Alex walked toward her, his movements stiff and awkward. "Katarina, I'm so sorry."

She could tell from the tone of Alex's voice that he didn't need any help in feeling rotten and she sniffed back her tears.

Looking at the fingernail moon still high in the sky, she realized they hadn't made as much progress as she'd hoped. She struggled to keep her frustration at bay. She didn't need to lash out at him, she repeated to herself. It could have happened to anyone.

"I just need to walk."

Alex took hold of her arm as she continued up the road. He turned on the flashlight, scanning their path.

"Katarina, stop!" He pulled her roughly to him in an unyielding embrace.

Struggling against him, she turned her head to see why he'd done so. Just ahead the road was washed away, leaving a six-foot drop.

Katarina gasped. "We...we...would have driven in there, Alex."

"Thank God. Thank God for that deer," he whispered, his breath hot against her ear.

She rested her head against Alex's chest and felt his heart pounding. A tumble of confusing thoughts and emotions assailed her. Her trembling limbs clung to him. "This must have been the road that was closed. Someone moved the detour sign."

Alex's rough hands rubbed her arms and held her securely. "Oh, Katarina."

She loved the sweet sound of him saying her name. Blood pounded in her brain and her knees trembled. She closed her eyes, blinking back tears.

Silently they both backed away and walked toward the car. Each time she picked up her pace, he did so also. *What's happening here? Get hold of yourself, Kat.* "We should call the state patrol," she said, her voice choked with emotion. "Where are we?" She found her phone on a tote and turned it on.

"Turned west at the detour between Cody and Meeteetse."

She held it in front of the headlight and looked at the readout. "No service."

There was one more ping from the car. Kat jumped back, then tossed her phone onto the pile of totes.

Katarina looked around for a bush and told Alex she'd be down the road for a few minutes. When she returned, he was spreading his sleeping bag out in the field.

"W-wait," she stammered. "What are you doing?" She pointed at the car, then back to Alex. "Maybe it'll still work."

"I can't fix this. The frame is probably twisted. Just look at it." He shrugged. "We'll have to go for help in the morning. Go ahead and take the sleeping bag. I'll stretch out over there."

"But…"

"There's no way to tell you how sorry I am, Katarina. For now, though, we may as well get some sleep."

Katarina pressed the light button on her watch and winced. "How far is it to the nearest town? I can't just sit here and do nothing."

"I'm afraid you'll have to. It's too far to walk tonight. We're better off staying here."

She looked around. He was right—there wasn't a light to be seen. Only the stars twinkling in the darkness. Her car rested in the distance and gasoline fumes still lingered in the air.

Alex wiped his hands on his shirt. "Do you have any warmer clothes along? It gets pretty chilly out here."

"I wasn't going to the tundra, remember? I was following the mountain range and staying in some hotel that'll leave the lights on for me." She choked back her frustration, willing herself not to cry. "We're in the middle of a heat wave. I was going to need air-conditioning, not a heater." The tears won. "No, I didn't bring anything warm to wear!" She sniffed.

"Kat." He stepped closer and took her in his arms. He gently wiped the tear from her cheek. "I'm so sorry."

"But my interview. I have to make it to Spokane by Wednesday morning." She was afraid to open those totes and see if any of her dolls had survived unbroken.

"You can call them in the morning, see if they can give you a little more time. They'll understand."

"I already pushed the interview back as far as I could. They really wanted me there tomorrow—today, whenever Tuesday is."

"We'll do what we can to make it. I'll do everything I can to get you there on time. You'll have to trust me on that." His embrace loosened and Alex stepped back. "After a day like today, it makes you wonder if God has other plans, doesn't it?" He turned and walked to the car and turned out the lights.

She didn't respond. She couldn't believe God wouldn't want her to get this offer. *Why, God? What do You want from me?* She'd worked so long to make it possible. Spent most of her savings on the prototype mold. It *had* to work out.

Alex dug through the pile they'd retrieved from the car and returned a few minutes later with a pair of wool socks and a sweatshirt.

She rubbed her arms, not actually cold, but mentally, the chill wouldn't go away. "What do you mean, God may have other plans, Alex? Why wouldn't He want me to make this deal?"

He shook his head. "It was just a random thought. I didn't mean anything by it." He tried again to hand her the clothes.

"I need this contract."

Alex let his hand drop to his side. "I never said you didn't. But sometimes our prayers aren't answered in quite the way we want them to be. God knows what we need, even before we ask. He also makes it very clear that He'll provide for our needs. Just like tonight, Katarina."

"So I'm just supposed to sit around and wait on Him? I don't think so." It wasn't a question, and she really didn't want Alex to answer. It didn't matter what he said. There were limits to what she could expect from others—including God. She'd learned that a long time ago. "Don't worry about me. I'll find a way to that interview."

Chapter Nine

Katarina slipped the sweatshirt over her sundress and held her arms out. The sleeves dangled like wings from her fingertips. A soft giggle escaped. "I don't think I'm going to need your sleeping bag after all."

"I wouldn't bet on it. Here, you'll need these, too."

She accepted the wool socks, stood on her tiptoes and gave him a kiss on the cheek. "Thank you, Alex. I'm really sorry about the way everything turned out today." Katarina rushed over to the sleeping bag and sat down while he stood there feeling as if his emotions had just been struck by lightning.

Alex pulled his nylon sleep sack from his bag and stuffed the liner inside, then stretched out on the grass nearby and turned his back to her. He wondered what she'd have done if he'd wrapped his arms around her and kissed her properly? *Engaged or not, you're far too irresistible to let another chance slip past.*

He heard the rustle of Katarina tossing and turning. "You okay?"

No answer.

"Katarina?" Alex raised himself up on his elbows. In the moonlight he could see her sit up. He raised his voice and repeated her name. "What are you doing?"

A timid voice whispered, "Trying to find how to zip the sleeping bag."

"I forgot all about that," he mumbled.

"What?" She cocked her head toward him, and he realized she couldn't hear him.

Suddenly everything was different. Unable to stop the feelings of protectiveness, he scooted over to her. "It needs a new zipper put in, and I forgot all about it. Here, let me help. Did you take your hearing aid out, or did it fall out during the accident?"

"I took it out. I can't sleep with it in. Sorry."

"No problem. I forgot is all."

After a few minutes the two of them were able to free the tab, but they still had to get the teeth lined up properly so it would close. He put the miniflashlight in his mouth to hold it so he could see.

"Alex, you're going to break a tooth. Don't do that! Here, I'll hold it for you."

Alex wiped the moisture from the handle onto his

shirt and handed it to her. Katarina leaned close to watch.

Despite the long day they'd had, he could still smell the faint scent of her perfume. He wasn't sure how much more temptation he could withstand.

"Why do they have separating zippers on them? Wouldn't it be easier to have it come to a stop at the bottom?"

"They're made to zip two of them together to make a double bed."

There was an awkward silence, followed by a very sheepish "Oh."

He wrestled with the zipper, trying to avoid looking at the pretty young woman inhabiting his sleeping bag. Just as he was ready to move the fabric, she did it, and the zipper teeth gripped one another. "What a team." Alex raised his hand, and she gave him a high five.

He could feel the warmth of her laughter on his neck.

"I've never been camping. I guess that's obvious."

"You're a great sport, considering this wasn't supposed to be a camping trip. It's quite a bit different with the right supplies. Lie down and I'll zip you in." He knelt next to her head and pulled the tab toward him. "Kzzzzt," rasped the zipper. He started to move back to his sack.

"Alex?"

"What?"

"Would you mind moving over to this side, so I can hear you?"

That protective instinct kicked in again and he fought it away. *The lady doesn't want a father, remember?*

Despite the warning going off in his head, he moved.

Where did he draw that line between what a man instinctively did for a woman, and what was "fatherly"? What kind of man was her fiancé? And didn't she realize the traits of a husband and father complemented one another? Didn't she want a husband who would make a good father to her children one day?

"Do you like fighting fires?"

The change of topic stopped him cold. It was a straightforward question. So why was he having to think about it? A moment later he finally answered. "Yeah, I do. As with any job, it has its drawbacks."

"You mean marriage?"

"That's one of them." His voice felt raw and gravelly, and he forced himself to move away.

"Surely all smokejumpers aren't single, are they?"

"No, there are some who take a chance on matrimony." *Don't ask so many questions, Katarina. I don't have all the answers.*

She quieted for a few minutes, then continued chattering nervously. "What's it like at a fire?"

"Fast, furious and hotter than hades," he answered honestly, hoping she'd drop the subject. Considering how he'd had to drag conversation from her all day, this sudden willingness to become friends took some getting used to. He wondered if she could see him watching her.

"No wonder the heat didn't bother you today."

He didn't know how to respond. He didn't want to discuss anything remotely related to work. That seemed a lifetime ago. "You warm enough?"

"I'm okay. What I would love is to have just a bit of that warm air back. Aren't you freezing?"

He paused. "This is a special fabric that holds in the heat," he said, lying through his chattering teeth. The space blanket that was supposed to hold in body heat wasn't doing a thing to help, either.

"Wow. Pretty amazing stuff. Looks like flannel."

It is. He wanted to chuckle so badly he almost choked.

She was quiet for less than a minute. "Tell me more about smoke jumping."

He moved closer to her. "Kat, we're perfectly safe."

"It's that obvious, huh? I hoped talking might take my mind off everything. Do you always sleep under the stars?"

"When I'm not close enough to a camp, I do." She listened while Alex told her about his accident and the fire that had claimed his friends. "I'm a perfect candidate for smoke jumping," he said cynically. "No commitments, no family. No one left behind to suffer the loss."

She was silent for a minute. "You're wrong, Alex." Her voice sounded weary, as if she might finally find the peace to rest.

Hope rose within him.

"You have a wonderful family who would miss you very much."

His heart slammed against his chest. Her admission wasn't at all what he'd hoped. What had he truly expected? They'd known each other only a few days. He didn't say anything, and at last she closed her eyes.

Katarina's head throbbed, but it was nothing compared to her heart. Why had God allowed this to happen? All of her dreams were disappearing before her eyes.

She sniffed, then tucked her face into the crook of her arm, hoping Alex hadn't heard. It had been a long time since either of them had said anything. *He's probably asleep by now.*

"Katarina? What's wrong?"

"It's nothing." Just hearing his voice was comforting. *You wanted adventure, Katarina, and look what you got.*

"You hit your head. Maybe I should check for signs of a concussion." He reached over to her and ran his hand through her fine hair, feeling for a bump.

"No." She turned away from him and tried to pull her hands out, to stop Alex, but the sleeves of his sweatshirt still covered her hands and were tangled somewhere underneath her body as she curled up to keep warm.

"Let me check your eyes, just in case." He turned the flashlight on and gave her a minute to prepare.

"There's nothing wrong with me, Alex. Just a little headache and a drippy nose."

"Can't hurt to check them anyway," he suggested. Alex gently opened each eye one at a time. "They look fine. Are you feeling sick? Nauseous? Dizzy?"

"I'm fine. Just aches and pains from the seat belt, I suppose. I can't believe He let all this happen."

"He? You mean God?"

She didn't answer. After all, who was she to question God? Katarina sniffed again.

"He charged His guardian angels to protect us." Alex shone the light on the crinkled-up car. "Praise the Lord we weren't hurt. I still can't quite believe we walked away from that. It could have been so much worse."

Katarina closed her eyes. She turned to one side, away from him and the car, frightened by the closeness that was developing between them. She'd never experienced a friendship like this with any other man. Was it the trauma of the day, or something more?

She was usually the one to see the glass half-full instead of half-empty. Yet Alex was the one pointing out how God had protected them, while she fought the temptation to blame Him for allowing the accident to happen in the first place.

She struggled to understand why her relationship with God was so difficult for her. Why she saw things so differently than most people. Where others felt comfort, she felt guilt. Others were grateful, and she felt unworthy. Cherished, she felt…abandoned.

Alex woke the next morning to the sound of a diesel truck barreling down the washboard road, and he jumped up to catch the trucker's attention. Both for help and for the driver's protection, in case the road sign hadn't been changed.

Katarina rolled over and looked up at him. "Alex. What's going on? Is help here?" Katarina reached into her purse. A minute later she put her hearing aid in.

He looked at the orange truck and back to Kat. "Looks like a highway department truck is coming. I'm going to see if he can call the state patrol on his radio. It'll be a while till a wrecker arrives. You okay?"

"I'll be fine."

He smiled, recalling their sporadic conversations during the night. "Snuggle back in, it's still pretty chilly out here." With each noise, Katarina had stirred, asking Alex which animal it was. Little did she know he'd struggled with his own questions until three in the morning, until he'd heard Katarina's breathing deepen. Before he fell asleep, he prayed that God would help him find the answers.

Alex walked up the embankment to the road and flagged the truck to a stop.

The driver glanced at the car and Katarina crawling out of the sleeping bag. "Looks like you've got quite a mess here. Everyone okay?"

Alex nodded, admiring how cute Katarina looked in her ankle-length yellow sundress, wool socks and his forest-green sweatshirt. "Fine. We need a wrecker."

The trucker looked at the car and back to Alex. "You know how lucky you are?"

He nodded. "We saw the washout up the road. Looks like some kids thought it would be funny to move the Road Closed sign, huh?"

"Patrolman saw it about midnight and moved it back. Must have just missed you."

"And he didn't check to see if anyone had run off the road?" Alex grunted in disgust. "Never mind. Would you call us a tow truck?"

"Sure. Need anything else?"

"We have food, but some hot coffee would be welcome."

While they waited, the rest of the crew and their assorted equipment arrived. Katarina and Alex assessed the damage and cleaned her personal things from the car.

He had asked himself a dozen times how he'd let himself care so much for an engaged woman. Especially one nearly a decade younger. It wasn't even so much her age that concerned him. She wanted the adventure she'd never experienced, and he wanted to settle down and start a family before it was too late, which she apparently thought it already was.

He'd had his fill of adventure, spending summers in some of the most beautiful forests of the country. He'd seen the best there was to see, areas few people ever had the chance to enjoy, and from a vantage point that even fewer could appreciate.

Two hours later, the wrecker arrived, along with the state trooper. The mechanic assured Katarina that the car was a loss, as the frame had been twisted.

There wasn't a place in town to rent, beg, borrow, or buy a vehicle. The bus wouldn't be back through town until the next morning, too late for her interview. Alex thought Katarina would break down, but she'd held strong.

Alex called a retired smokejumper who lived nearby. John was glad to give them a lift to the nearest city.

By the time they'd filled out the reports, driven with John to the city and rented a car, it was well past noon. They pulled into Alex's driveway late that afternoon. Alex unlocked the door and motioned Katarina inside. "You go ahead and clean up while I check my mail and make some phone calls. There's a Whirlpool tub in my room, if you'd like to relax a while. It's old, but still works the knots out."

"Ah-ha." Her face lit up. "Now I see why you still look as young as you did when we first met."

Alex groaned as he carried the last of her totes inside. "Tell my thirty-five-year-old body that."

She blushed.

He escorted her to the guest room, then led the way upstairs and showed her the Jacuzzi controls.

Alex returned downstairs to his office and listened to his phone messages, then checked his e-mail as he sorted the mail. He called Kevin to tell him about the trip.

A few minutes later, Katarina showed up in his office and he told Kevin to hold on. "Katarina, what are you doing here already? You're supposed to sit in there and relax. I guarantee, that takes more than five minutes."

"How am I supposed to relax when I'm drowning in bubbles?"

"Drowning in bubbles? How did that happen?"

"An opened shampoo bottle fell in the tub."

He started laughing and fell against the wall. "I don't believe this."

When he picked up the phone, Emily was on the line, frantic to know if her younger sister was okay. "She's fine." He started laughing again. "Unless you consider drowning oneself in bubbles a problem.''

After a mock scolding, Emily put Kevin back on the line and Alex explained to his brother what had happened and they both started laughing again. From the other room he heard a soft feminine voice yell, ''It's not funny!''

''Before I forget, Kevin—'' Alex lowered his voice ''—I need to ask if there's a problem with my spending a while longer here. I need to get a few things settled.''

He heard Katarina enter the office. She was wearing another soft, flowing dress that he was coming to accept as totally Katarina. Totally feminine. Absolutely beautiful.

''I'm not sure how long I'll need to stay.'' He tried to concentrate on his conversation with Kevin. How could he discriminate what God had planned for him with Katarina so close? Everything had happened so quickly. ''I'll do what I can. Ask Emily if she'd like to talk to the mermaid.''

He handed the phone to Katarina, along with a gentle pat on the shoulder. ''I'll be back down in a few minutes.''

Alex hurried through his shower and tried to ignore thoughts of Katarina. It was useless. He stubbed his toe on her overnight bag, then nicked his chin with the razor.

She confused him as no other woman ever had. On the one hand, she insisted she was going to marry Ron, and yet hinted that Alex needed to find a woman who liked traveling. She didn't understand. Jumping and marriage weren't mutually compatible. He'd seen what following a jumper did to a woman. It wasn't fair to ask that of anyone.

Alex had no doubt in his mind that he'd be happy back with Kevin's construction company. He liked the hours, and the idea that he could finally settle down. *Question is, Father, is that Your plan, or mine?*

Losing his closest friend hadn't done this to him. No matter how often he reminded himself that even before the accident he'd been thinking it was time for a change, Alex felt leaving the jumpers now was a cop-out.

It wasn't fear that made him look at his friend's widow and realize what he had to give up to continue jumping. Yes, he loved fire fighting. He loved the challenge, and the responsibility. He just didn't want to think of the woman he loved going through what other wives and ex-wives did. Even though he knew his reasons for considering leaving were valid, he still wasn't sure it was the right decision for him.

And now there was Katarina. The woman who proved that love at first sight was real.

Chapter Ten

Katarina was on the phone when Alex came downstairs cleaned up and freshly shaven. "I'm fine, Ron. I'll make it in plenty of time." She smiled at Alex and held up a finger, motioning that she'd just be another minute.

Thankfully, Alex waited in the kitchen while she finished her conversation. She hung up the receiver and walked down the hall to join him. He stepped into the doorway just as she did and she took a step back.

Had he overheard their conversation? Had he heard the irritation in her voice when they'd said goodbye? "I used my phone card to call Ron."

"You didn't have to. Should have just dialed direct."

Katarina shrugged. *Alex and Ron are total opposites.* In the same way Alex opened up to people,

Ron kept a tight rein on his privacy. Alex was generous, and Ron a shrewd businessman. "He phoned Emily three times last night, upset that I hadn't called him."

"Guess he'd better get over it. We did the best we could." He squeezed past her to turn out the office light.

Katarina looked at Alex. "You don't like him, do you?"

Alex leaned one shoulder on the door frame and crossed his arms over his chest, his muscles fighting the constraints of his sleeves. "No."

She was shocked by the lack of hesitation in Alex's reply. "You've never even met him. How can you make that kind of judgment?"

"I don't like anyone who steals that smile from your face. Yesterday I didn't like myself much either," he said without pause.

Katarina hesitated, momentarily baffled. Her heartbeat quickened, and she found herself breathing faster. "That kind of comment, Alex MacIntyre, could get you into a heap of trouble."

One side of his mouth curved into a resigned smile as he raised an eyebrow. "I think I already am." Standing upright, he stepped closer. "I'm starved. What do you say we find a steak house for supper?"

Katarina paused. "Fine."

Alex helped Katarina into the cab of his truck. "What is it about you guys and gargantuan trucks?"

"We have off-road jobs, Katarina. We need trucks that can take a beating. Not to mention, they're a lot more fun in the mud." He pressed the garage door opener and backed the truck past her rental car and into the street.

She laughed. "I'll trust your word on that. I've had way too much excitement for this week."

"After we eat, we'll go over the map. When do you need to leave?"

"Ah," she teased. "You changed your mind about taking me yourself, huh?"

For an instant Alex was tempted to take on her silent challenge, but he knew better than to fall prey to temptation. He needed time to himself, where he could hear God's answers to his many questions. "Sorry, but I need to get things settled here."

Katarina's smile was sweet and understanding. "I know. I can't tell you how thankful I am you were with me yesterday."

He laughed. "You'd know I was lying if I said I enjoyed it. But I did enjoy getting to know you."

They were seated in a corner booth at the best steak house in Missoula, complete with peanut shells on the floor. They were actually able to laugh about the rotten day they'd survived together, from the overheated car to spraying her with ice-cold water to freezing and talking the night away.

Katarina hit him playfully when he confessed that he'd been as cold as she. Her laugh was contagious.

"I didn't think that fabric looked any different, but then, it was dark. And to think, I *trusted* you." She giggled some more.

Her eyes were full of life, pain and unquenchable warmth. She wore her sense of humor like a shield, protecting herself from life's painful moments. Alex longed to know everything about her, to help Katarina heal her pain, to carry her burdens.

"That wasn't so difficult, was it?" he asked gently. "Trusting me, I mean."

The expression in her big blue eyes seemed to plead for friendship. Not just the superficial kind she was used to, but the kind that bound friends together forever—that turned friends into husband and wife. She didn't answer.

Father, am I deceiving myself? Is Katarina in love with Ron? Or have You saved her for me? Alex took a deep breath. "I didn't mean to be so pushy. Forgive me." By the end of dinner they were both wearing down. Had he burned his chances with her, or was it exhaustion? Whatever the reason, it proved that putting space between himself and Katarina was the best thing for both of them.

They returned to Alex's condo. Alex pulled out a map of the area and highlighted the route she should take to Spokane and then back to Springville.

"I should leave now, just in case."

"You don't believe in 'just in cases,' remember? You'll do fine."

A small, tentative smile seemed all she could muster.

Alex leaned against the counter and crossed his arms over his chest, fighting the urge to take her in his arms and calm her unspoken fears. After yesterday, he was sure there were several of them. "I think the best thing for you is a good night of sleep."

"I am tired. I need to be there by eleven, so I should be okay if I leave by six, right?"

"I'll set my alarm to fix breakfast and see you off."

Thankfully, the return trip was nothing like the drive to Montana. Road construction seemed confined to the northbound lane, the heat wave was over and the rental car ran perfectly. Still, she was exhausted.

Katarina pressed the doorbell and waited for Emily to answer. The windows were open, and it smelled as if her sister had been baking.

"Kat? Why are you ringing the doorbell? Did you lose your key?" Emily answered, then stepped back to let her inside. Slinging Ricky over his shoulder, Kevin stood in the foyer and smiled.

"No, I didn't lose my key. Seems the only thing I haven't lost in the past few days. I didn't want to walk right in." She said hello to Ricky and Kevin.

He lowered his son to the ground and stepped out the door. "Hi, Kat. You need help unloading?"

"Don't bother. I just stopped by to pick up some fresh clothes and find out the arrangements with Mrs. Simmons. I did get the apartment, didn't I?" Katarina strode past her sister, hoping to put the past few days behind her.

From the corner of her eye she saw Emily shake her head at Kevin. "Wait a minute. How did the meeting go?" Emily looked at her watch. "I didn't expect you for at least two more days. What happened?"

Katarina swallowed hard. "There was no meeting," she said, struggling to remain calm. "Life goes on. I need to get settled into a place of my own. Did Mrs. Simmons drop the key off?"

Emily looked at Kevin nervously. "Wait a minute."

"Emily, this has been a really lousy week. Don't make it worse. You didn't tell her no, did you?" Kat looked from Emily to Kevin, unconsciously holding her breath.

Emily hesitated, then nodded. "Sit down, Kat...."

"How could you?" Tears burned her tired eyes. It was time she put the past few days and all of her pipe dreams aside and faced reality. How could Emily turn on her?

"We have a terrific plan. Don't get upset." Emily wrapped her arm around Katarina and brushed the hair from her face. "You're going to love it."

Kevin stepped forward and handed Katarina a set of keys. "Here, we thought my house would work better. I don't want to sell it quite yet. It has plenty of room, and I don't want it sitting empty, especially with summer just starting.''

She stared at her brother-in-law. ''It was a nice thought, Kevin, and I appreciate your offer, but I can't afford to rent a huge house. Not to mention, there's already someone living in it. And I'm *not* interested in seeing your brother again.'' Katarina handed the keys back.

Kevin furrowed his brows. ''What did Alex do?''

Emily led Katarina to the sofa. ''Sit down. Tell us what happened.''

Katarina resigned herself to losing any upcoming argument, plopped herself on the couch and closed her eyes. Was it only four days ago that she'd left here, hopeful that her life was about to change forever? She would never in her wildest dreams have imagined that the week would turn out like this.

She took a deep breath. ''When I stopped for gas yesterday, I called Bearly Toys to confirm directions to their office. They'd changed my appointment to Tuesday afternoon.''

''But that's crazy. They only called Monday morning.''

''They said they'd tried to call my cell phone Tuesday after meeting with another designer, to give me one last chance to meet. By yesterday morning they had already signed a contract, with someone else.''

Emily wrapped her arms around Katarina and

gave her a long hug. "If that's the kind of business they run, you don't need to deal with them."

Katarina groaned. "You sound just like Alex." Just saying his name sent her into confusion again. For the past eight hundred miles she'd done little besides try to reason through what exactly had happened between them.

One minute she detested him, then before she knew it, they'd become friends, and now… Well, now nothing made any sense at all. Suddenly her heart was fluttering and she was short of breath.

"When's Uncle Alex coming back?" Ricky chimed in.

Trying to keep the irritation from her voice, Katarina took another breath and exhaled. "I don't know, honey. I didn't discuss that with him."

Kevin patted his son on the bottom, "Ricky, why don't you go get a snack? I think I saw some of our favorite Snickerdoodles on the counter."

As soon as Ricky was gone, Kevin lowered his voice as if expecting something vile to have happened. "What about Alex? What did he do?"

"He came along, for starters." Katarina tapped her index finger on her opposite hand, listing their mishaps. "There was the road construction. The engine overheated." She took a deep breath and ticked off Alex's numerous transgressions. "So to avoid all the construction, he took me on some wild-goose chase across Wyoming. He has an opinion about everything from cars to dolls. He even had the nerve to tell me just what it takes to be sure you've found the right person to marry, and *then* he managed to run my car into the ground. We were stranded in the middle of absolutely *nowhere*. Your brother is the pushiest man I've ever met!'' Katarina stood and began pacing. Just talking about their disastrous trip made her mad all over again. ''If we had stayed on the interstate, I wouldn't have missed that phone call. So I made the entire trip for nothing, not to mention I now have no car.''

No one said a word. She caught Emily trying to wipe a smile from her face as she and Kevin exchanged glances.

''Then your brother also had the nerve to say that maybe all these mishaps are a sign from God that this isn't meant to be. I could strangle him.''

''I'm sure God has something better in the works, Kat.''

Katarina threw up her hands and let out a cynical laugh. ''Not you, too. God's will must be for me to be miserable.'' Katarina combed the hair from her face. Her hand paused by her ear. ''I would have thought you'd be a little more understanding.''

''I do understand.'' Emily's smile softened. ''I'm sorry about the interview and the car. But I'm still so thankful He was with you two, and that you're both okay,'' Emily said, echoing Alex's sentiments. ''You're tired, Katarina.''

''I'm fine,'' she argued, even though she didn't feel fine. Her entire world had been tumbled and tossed up in the air these past few days. Only problem was, she had to figure out just how all those pieces were going to fit back together again.

Katarina couldn't look at Kevin.

"Humph, so that's what this is all about," Kevin said, then added, "I don't expect Alex to be back for a while, in case you want to reconsider staying at the house."

"He's not coming back?" Her voice rose an octave. "I'm so sorry, Kevin, it's all my fault."

Emily's eyebrows arched, and Katarina realized she'd just stuck her foot into her mouth again. Kevin and Emily looked at each other with questions hanging between them.

Katarina didn't need more speculation...from anyone. If Alex wasn't going to come back, there was no point in refusing their generous offer. Doing so would only make matters worse. Katarina had invested more money into her business, anticipating expanding production. Between unexpected expenses from the trip and the accident, her entire savings had now been depleted. She had precious little money to put down a deposit on an apartment and replace the dolls damaged in the car accident.

Tears formed as she thought of it all again. Katarina rubbed her eyes. She had to do a better job of covering her emotions. She had to stop reacting to Alex. There was only one way to keep all their questions at bay—pretend. Pretend Alex's presence did nothing to her. Pretend she had no doubts about her and Ron. Pretend everything was fine, even though that couldn't be further from the truth.

Kevin closed the gap between them. "Katarina, this is what family is for. We help each other when the going gets rough, just like Alex running the company for me. And you're my sister now. I expect to help out however I can. I want you to stay at the house as long as you need to."

"If the house is going to be empty anyway, I may as well consider it. As long as you wouldn't mind if I look for someone to share the rent, until Ron and I get married, anyway."

Kevin handed her the key again and she sat back down on the sofa. Emily and Kevin joined her. "It'll be rent free until we get my things out of it, so don't worry about finding someone immediately. Until I finish the clinic project, I doubt we'll have time to do much. Especially without Alex's help."

From the tone of Kevin's voice, Katarina could tell he wasn't happy with the latest turn of events where it involved his brother. He needed Alex's help. She hated to admit it, but she, too, was more disappointed than happy that Alex wouldn't be coming back.

Still, she felt guilty taking advantage of her brother-in-law's generosity. "I don't know, Kevin. I don't feel right taking it rent free, but maybe I could do something to help out, in trade for rent...."

Just then, Ricky wandered into the room with peanut butter and jelly all over the front of him. "Why don't you ask God what to do? He knows everything.''

Kevin opened his arms to his son, not seeming to mind the mess at all. ''I tell you what, why don't we pray, and I'm sure things will turn out perfectly.''

The suggestion stopped her cold. *Pray? About a house?*

Emily reached out her hands, Ricky and Kevin took hold immediately, and the three waited for Katarina. Finally she joined hands, completing the circle.

''Our Father,'' Kevin began, ''we're told not to be anxious about anything, but to turn to You with our needs and prayers.''

Without missing a beat, Emily took over. ''We ask for Katarina to feel at peace, Lord. You know better than we do what all of our needs are and will be in the coming months, and we ask for Your direction. We praise You for the many blessings You've surprised us with this past few weeks, Father. Though we don't always understand Your ways, I thank You for always being there to listen when we need comfort and answering our needs according to Your will.''

There was a long silence before Ricky whispered, ''Is it my turn?''

''Sure,'' his daddy whispered back.

''And thank you, God, for taking care of Auntie

Kat and Uncle Alex, and please bring him back here wif us really fast. Amen.''

''Amen,'' echoed Kevin and Emily.

Katarina clenched her jaw to curb the sob in her throat. She folded her hands and focused her gaze on them.

''Kevin, would you mind helping Ricky clean up?'' Emily asked.

Kevin patted Katarina's shoulder, and he and Ricky went upstairs in silence.

''Katarina?''

Katarina swallowed hard and buried her face in her hands to avoid Emily's gaze. ''I don't want to talk.''

''About anything?'' Emily's voice was soft.

She shook her head.

''Okay, then, just listen. I've wanted to tell you this for a while now, but it never seemed to be the right time.'' Emily cleared her throat. ''God knows you're mad at our dad for leaving, and He's everything Karl Berthoff couldn't be.''

Katarina felt the sobs break loose, and could no longer hold them back. ''How…did…you know?''

''I've always known, Kat. You were daddy's little girl and his leaving broke your heart.'' She brushed the hair off Katarina's face. ''You're a hopeless romantic. You never gave up hope that he and Mom would get back together. And yet you fight letting people love you more than anyone I know. Including God. God doesn't like what our earthly father did to hurt us. But you have to trust that God will never leave you. You are His precious child, Kat.''

''I sure don't feel very precious right now.''

''In Proverbs it says 'Trust in the Lord with all thine heart, and lean not unto thine own understanding. In all thy ways acknowledge Him, and He shall direct thy paths.''' She took Kat's hand and squeezed it. ''Enough for now. Get some rest— you'll feel better in the morning.''

''Yes, Mother,'' Katarina said sarcastically, then gave her sister a hug. ''I suppose I can handle one night with the newlyweds.''

''Newlywed *parents*. That changes everything.''

Katarina smiled, drying the tears from her cheeks. ''I'm so happy for you and Kevin, Emily. It's like your world always should have been.''

''That's my Pollyanna. Welcome home, Kat.''

The next few days were a whirlwind of activity. Katarina moved into Kevin's house, ignoring the fact that all of his belongings were still in their original place. She set up her things in a spare bedroom on the main floor. She replaced the geometric-design bedding with her own hand-quilted coverlet. By adding a sash of coordinating colors to the vertical blinds, Katarina changed the entire appearance of the room. In the corner she placed her grandmother's armoire, which she'd converted to a cabinet to hold a small television and the computer.

Kevin and one of his builders set her kiln in the

garage temporarily and moved her painting table into the unfinished basement along with the inventory. The sewing machine and fabrics were in the room across the hall from her bedroom and office. It was time to get back to work.

The phone rang, and Katarina picked it up just as the answering machine clicked on. Hearing her younger sister's voice on the other end was as soothing as a chocolate delicacy. "Where are you now?" Katarina curled up with the pillows on her bed and listened while Lisa told her about her latest magazine assignment in Missouri. "Oh, I feel so sorry for you. Last week Hawaii, this week Missouri, poor dear," she said, laughing. "Yes, my trip was horrible, and then I didn't even get the job." Katarina confirmed what Lisa had heard from Emily. "The man's...presumptuous."

Lisa read between the lines.

Katarina felt a smile and a blush spread across her face. "So what if he's adorable?" Her mind returned to the accident, and the tenderness of Alex's protective embraces, missing her sister's next remark.

Katarina punched the pillow. She *had* to take her mind off Alex MacIntyre.

"What did you say, Lisa? I uh...dropped the phone."

Lisa repeated her question.

"Emily said what?"

Katarina twirled the cord around her finger, then struggled to get it off.

"He's off fighting fires, Lisa. Nothing—*nothing* is going to become of us, so save that imagination of yours for your articles."

Chapter Eleven

"Ready?"

Alex nodded. "Let's do it."

"Get in the door!" the spotter yelled.

Alex hooked up the static line, completed his four-point check and braced himself. Smoke billowed from the pristine forest as if funneled through a pine smokestack. He stepped up to the doorway of the DC-3 and looked again at the jump spot. "Looks like a fun one."

His partner smiled. "Just so we make it through those goalposts."

Alex spotted the pair of seventy-foot ponderosa pines that Gary referred to. Going between them sure beat hitting the boulders to the lee side, or the fire on the other.

"Clear!"

Alex stepped out and seconds later felt the parachute deploy. *Wow, God. This is beautiful.*

He looked at the yellow, white and blue canopy above him, then steered between the uprights. The landing went smoothly. He hit, rolled, then ripped his helmet off and turned to watch Gary's landing. Four jumpers followed in tandem.

The crew worked for thirty-six hours digging line, trying to stay ahead of the fire. The wind changed direction twice, chasing them into the black, eating up the ground in its path. He was bone weary and couldn't wait for a break.

It was after a two-hour nap in the middle of the safety of the burned forest floor that the intensity of his feelings for Katarina hit him. *Why can't I put her out of my mind, God? I beg You to take these feelings away. There's no way we could ever make it work. This is no life to offer a woman. And she's made it clear she wants nothing to do with me.*

He took his frustration out on the downed logs, sawing through them and throwing them into the burn. When that was through, he took out his Pulaski and started building a hand line around the area.

Alex had struggled for the better part of two weeks trying to ignore the voice in his head that continued to quote the Bible verse from Jeremiah, "For I know the plans I have for you." *A future and a hope.* With Katarina? Or here, in the woods? Alex looked around at the land he'd come to love.

The forests and hills, blue skies and rivers. They had brought him comfort through the years. But no more.

Attempts to convince himself that jumping again would solve everything were nothing more than a cruel joke.

When Katarina left for Spokane, he'd gone to the doctor and received the clearance necessary to return to work, then completed his annual refresher course requirements. With each step, he'd prayed for peace that returning for another season was the right decision.

The push-ups, sit-ups and pull-ups hadn't been any problem, but there'd been a moment of pause before the one-and-a-half-mile run. He'd gutted it out, reassured that it would all be over in less than eleven minutes. Back on the job, he'd been sure the adrenaline rush from the fires would spur him on. It hadn't.

Even being out on a fire, he couldn't keep his mind off family. Or the lack thereof. After the fire assessment and that initial rush to get it under control, there was still time to remember what he was missing back in Colorado. Time to think of the years past. To wonder how the family would celebrate Kevin's Fourth of July birthday. He'd missed all those family gatherings for the past eight summers. Missed watching his nephews growing up. Missed the chance to meet his niece before fire had taken her life.

Each day for the past two weeks, Alex had tried to regain that familial camaraderie with the other jumpers. Whether bunking in the dorms or sleeping in the ash, he wondered what pulled him back year after year.

This crew was a mixture of new and old faces. A new season. "War stories" were enthusiastically passed from one generation to the next.

While preparing freeze-dried spaghetti, Don Brown, an old friend, slapped him on the back. "I'm sure Alex has at least one story to tell."

He took a deep breath of the stale smoke-filled air and swallowed another mouthful of bottled water, trying to rekindle the zeal to share his experiences with this new crop of recruits. Eager eyes rested on him, and he managed, somehow, to retell the story of his broken ankle. "Four of us jumped into steep terrain covered with rocks, downed trees and snag. Lighting was bad." He took another drink of water. "All of a sudden, this gnarly old log jumped into my path from the shadows. My foot caught on it, and sucked me down. I thought I'd sprained it. So I stood up to pull in my canopy. Fell flat on my face."

The men chuckled, egging him on.

"Days like that, you realize real quick that God is in control. The weather was squirrelly—wind chased us, and suddenly our window was closing. I didn't even have time to say a whole prayer." Alex paused. *Your Father knows what you need before you ask.* "Never forget, fellows, you're not out here alone. That fire died down long enough for them to help me to a clearing and get me out of there." He stretched out his foot, ignoring the stiffness from a hard day's work. "Good as new." Alex unlaced his boots and tugged each one off.

When the campfire was out, he crawled into the sleeping bag covered with soot and looked up at the stars. Katarina came to mind immediately. Alex closed his eyes and prayed. The sense of failure had a strong hold on him. "God, I can't tell if what I want to do is Your answer to my prayers, or simply temptation luring me away from You. I need Your guidance, Father."

After the few weeks spent helping Kevin on the job, he realized what he was missing. His life felt empty because it *was* empty. Despite what Katarina had said, no one cared whether he came home each night. He ate dinner alone, or worse, in a mess tent full of dead-tired firefighters who smelled worse than the fires they battled.

He missed his family. Not to mention the spunky lady who'd set his emotions on fire. *She's committed to someone else, Father. Why can't I shake this feeling?* In his heart he knew better than to doubt the message God was sending him, but in his mind he kept hearing Kat tell him to stop trying to be a father to her. *I don't know how to care for you, Katarina Berthoff, but I guarantee you, trying to be your father is not my intention.*

He could still see her in that ultrafeminine yellow sundress. Feel the disappointment each time he heard her claim she *would* marry the "Boy Scout." The human side of him acknowledged the totally ungodly side that was as green with jealousy as a meadow in the spring. But for the life of him, he couldn't stop it.

Alex had gone to college, planning to take over his father's business one day. When that day came, he'd been too overcome with grief to stick around. He'd run. *I had other plans for you, Alex. Don't be ashamed.* Was this chance to help Kevin opportunity knocking? A chance to go back and right the wrongs in his past? A chance to follow his dreams? Or his dreams running away with his hopes?

The next morning the crew packed out at first light. Their food rations were gone. Each carried a hundred pounds to the county road, where a bus took them back to the base. When they arrived, Alex cleaned up, then picked up a couple of lukewarm breakfast burritos from the mess hall for himself and his boss. It was time to face the situation head-on. He knocked on the door and Greg's familiar bellow invited him inside.

"Hey there, stranger!"

Alex held up the sack and waited for his friend and supervisor, Greg Johannsen, to clear the paperwork from his desk before setting it down. "We need to talk."

"Pour yourself a cup of coffee and spill your guts.

What's the problem?'' Greg pushed his chair back and crossed one ankle over the opposite knee.

Pulling a disposable cup from the stack, Alex added a sprinkle of cream and sugar before pouring the piping-hot brew. The silence grew. ''I can't do this, Greg. I'm going to have to take some more time off.''

''What's her name?'' he said jokingly.

That was the problem with having a boss who was also a friend, Alex realized. ''I didn't...''

Greg laughed. ''You didn't have to say it. Nine out of ten times it's about a woman in this business. Either wanting one, or trying to keep one. Which is it?'' Greg took a bite and followed it with a swig of coffee.

Everyone was always trying to set Alex up. It was well-known in the tightly knit community of jumpers that unlike many, Alex refused to marry in the spring and say goodbye for six months. More than once, the woman he'd been seeing when fire season rolled around had moved on to greener pastures by fall. Alex took it as a sign—as long as he jumped, he'd stay single.

Leaving Greg's question unanswered, Alex moved on. ''I liked being back in construction. I liked the nine-to-five, going-home-at-night schedule. That kind of thing could grow on me at my age. It surprised me.''

''Sounds nice for a while,'' Greg added unconvincingly.

You know me too well. Alex took a bite and avoided his friend's probing gaze.

"The spark's gone, isn't it?" Greg stood, a heavy sigh escaping as he walked across the room.

Alex thought of the friends he'd lost the year before, and felt like a coward bailing out on them. "I'm not sure, to be honest. The best thing would be to take a leave of absence. I need to get things straight in my own mind."

"You do know we have a heat wave going on?" It was an instinctive response for a supervisor. He didn't mean it personally.

Alex nodded. "I've kept track of what's going on. I'm not totally out of the loop." So far they'd been lucky, and he knew it as well as everyone else. "I'm not saying I'm through forever. It may be a break is all I need."

Greg poured himself another cup of coffee and sat on the corner of his desk. "You talked to anyone?"

Alex knew exactly what his friend meant—a counselor. Had it not been for his own injury, he'd have been with his crew on that deadly fire. "Yeah, I talked to him. I'm okay. I'm just thinking it may be time to move on. I have no complaints, Greg. You know as well as I do, you have a good crew this year." Alex rattled on about the experience of the team as well as the returning seasonals, suddenly confident about his decision to take this chance. At peace with following God's will...

"And I repeat," his friend said with a wide grin, "what's her name?"

This time Alex laughed. "I'm telling you, there is no one."

"Don't give me that. I see that glint in your eye. The one that *used* to be there when we talked about fires." Greg chugged the last of his coffee and set his pottery mug on the desk. "All of a sudden you head back to civilization, then show up here saying you need time to figure out where your life is going." Greg paused and slapped Alex on the shoulder. "I hate to lose you, Alex. You know we'll miss you out there, but I know what you're going through. We all question the wisdom of jumping into infernos at some point. And…if it doesn't work out, there's always a job waiting for you."

Alex stood and reached out his hand. "You have my brother's number. Call if you need me."

Greg clutched Alex's hand and gave him a firm hug. "I'll be expecting a name to thank for bringing that spark back to your eye. Keep in touch."

Alex knew there were no guarantees. Katarina had a serious boyfriend and a strategic plan for her future, which was far more than he could claim at this point. Knowing Kevin, he could very well be looking for a job as well as a wife when he arrived. If nothing else, maybe Adam could use a hand running his ranch.

It had been a good long while since he'd played

cowboy, but he had no doubt that after a few saddle-sore days he'd be back in shape.

Alex tried Kevin again, to no avail. He tossed the last of his bags into the bed of his truck and locked the door behind him. *Okay, God, what's the plan?*

Her grandfather clock struck seven. Ron should have been here half an hour ago. He was never late.

Katarina had pushed to finish moving in, and things were as settled as they could be until Kevin cleared out completely. She had washed the sheets on his bed so Ron could stay in his room for the weekend. Katarina set up her own furnishings, which had been stored in Emily's garage for the past two months.

She looked at her watch again and stirred the beef Stroganoff, Ron's favorite meal. "Why do I do this? Why do I let him irritate me this way?" She refused to blow out the candles, convinced that he'd be here any time.

When the phone rang she snatched the receiver from the cradle and answered. Katarina paced the floor, anxious for Ron to finish his excuse. "To-morrow?" She couldn't help but be disappointed.

Ron's reason told her nothing. "You can't explain right now, which must mean you're at your parents', right?" She suspected his delay wasn't totally un-intentional. He probably wanted her to see just how he'd felt when she didn't call him from her trip.

After receiving the confirmation, she knew it was useless to try talking to him. "Is everyone okay?"

Another monosyllabic reply. He always clammed up around his mother and father, especially when it came to disagreements.

Katarina dissolved onto the sofa. "Tell them hello for me, and I'll see you in the morning, then." She closed her eyes and blinked away the pain.

She considered clearing the dishes from the table, then decided to leave them. They'd just set it again tomorrow, anyway. Maybe then Ron would realize the trouble she'd taken to make their visit special. She hadn't seen him in almost two months and was feeling very lonely.

He'd canceled his visit the weekend Emily and Kevin were married, claiming she'd be too busy and didn't need him to distract her. Though he was right, she had to admit, she was hurt that he didn't care to be part of her family's celebration.

Katarina decided to walk to Emily and Kevin's house to pick up any mail that might not have been forwarded. Going without a car had been great incentive to stay home and get back on schedule with her dolls. It had been days since she'd gone outside for more than to check the mail from the cluster box down the street.

She grabbed her house keys and looked back at the table as she walked out the door. Like clockwork, flowers had arrived this afternoon with Ron's name on the card. Alex's remark about the efficient secretary came to mind, and Katarina slammed the door.

Ron arrived the next morning, not a minute late. She watched his car pull up to the curb and suddenly felt apprehensive. *There's nothing to worry about, Katarina. This is Ron.* His curly black hair was cut shorter than usual, and he wore his usual khakis and polo shirt. He opened the back of his SUV, grabbed a small suitcase and closed the hatch.

He looked up and smiled with his usual confidence. "I'm here."

Katarina hoped her apprehension wasn't as apparent as it felt. "Hi. I've missed you."

"Yeah, me, too. We have some catching up to do."

She swallowed. "I'd say so—you've grown a goatee." She grinned. "It looks nice, very stylish."

Ron wrapped his arms around her waist and kissed her as if there wouldn't be another chance. "What do you think?"

Think?

He lifted her hand to his beard. "If you don't like it, I'll shave it off."

Stunned by his offer, Katarina shook her head. "No, I'm sure I'll get used to it. Come on in, let me show you around. You'll stay in the loft."

"Do you have a table for me to set up my laptop?"

"No, but maybe I can find one in Kevin's things."

He headed immediately to the dining-room table and pushed the flowers to one end with her grandmother's china.

"Not there, Ron. It's all ready for us to eat," Katarina protested.

He glanced at it a minute, then back to her. "It's okay, it won't take up much room. And this way, we can go over your books while we watch a movie."

He was oblivious. She resigned herself to sharing her romantic dinner with a movie and talk of investments and growth plans. "Great. What was I thinking?"

The weekend was uneventful. He kept up with his work, and suggested she stitch while they watched movies. Before he left Sunday evening, Ron took her to the grocery store to stock up, since she had no car.

He wanted to help her business succeed. He was only encouraging her to catch up on the work she'd missed while she'd been on that awful trip. It didn't really matter that they hadn't gotten around to an evening walk through the beautiful neighborhood, or talked about anything more revealing than whether she liked his beard. He *had been* considerate enough to offer to shave if it bothered her.

Katarina struggled with the disappointing aspects of his trip. She hoped next time he'd feel up to going to dinner with Kevin and Emily and Ricky. That they would have time to go to the mountains for the day. Something other than stay at home.

She tried to convince herself that it wasn't fair to compare Ron to Alex. So what if the house hadn't fallen down around them? There was more to life than excitement. Being with Ron was…comfortable and secure. But if Ron was exactly the kind of man she needed, why did she feel more confused than before?

Chapter Twelve

Alex turned the key and walked into the house.

"Emily?" Katarina's cheerful voice echoed from the beamed ceilings.

"Katarina?" he mumbled. *What's she doing here?* Alex glanced to the empty driveway and back toward the kitchen. Dinner smelled heavenly. The dining-room table was set for company, complete with a bouquet of flowers in the middle. *The Boy Scout strikes again.*

Katarina's voice rang out urgently. "Kevin?" There was a crash, followed by a yelp and the rush of water from the faucet. "Who's there?"

Alex cleared his throat to speak. He turned and looked at the door. This wasn't at all what he had expected. He didn't dare leave without saying something. If only Kevin had answered his phone last night. He dropped his bags and headed toward the kitchen.

"I don't know who..." Katarina rushed around the corner wielding a huge black pan over her head.

As she took a swing at him, Alex stopped it with one hand and wrapped the other around her so she didn't lose her balance. "Whoa."

"Alex?" Katarina gasped.

Still stunned that he'd just about been branded with a cast-iron skillet, he yanked the pan from her hands. "Hi. Welcome home would have been fine."

She stumbled back. "What are you doing here?"

"I might ask you the same thing."

Hands on her hips, Katarina straightened her shoulders and lifted her chin. "I live here. What's your explanation?"

He turned his back to her and muttered under his breath just as Kevin, Emily and Ricky walked through the front door.

The way everyone looked at him, you'd think he was a ghost returned from the dead, he thought. The only one who didn't appear confused was the little boy flying toward him. "Uncle Alex!"

Alex knelt to greet his nephew and swooped him into his arms. "Hey there, sport. How are you doing?"

"Great! I knew you'd come back," he insisted. He gave Alex another tight bear hug. "I just *knew* it."

He had obviously been the subject of more than one conversation in the past two weeks.

"Sorry, things took longer to clear up than I expected," Alex said, focusing on Kevin.

His brother had a half smile on his face. "I was beginning to wonder if you'd decided against helping me out after all. I thought you meant a couple extra days, not weeks. Where have you been?"

He couldn't go into everything now. "I'm sorry. I tried to leave messages when I could get to a phone, but your machine kept cutting me off. Why don't I fill you in tomorrow?"

Emily broke in by giving Alex a hug. "It's good to see you, Alex. Sorry about the answering machine. We replaced it this morning. I'm afraid Lego pieces don't agree with the machine's diet."

Ricky jumped into his daddy's arms and nuzzled Kevin's shoulder. "It's okay, Ricky. Mommy's teasing. Look at her smile."

"Katarina, can I help you in the kitchen? The Stroganoff smells delicious."

Alex looked over his shoulder to see Katarina turn and retreat into the kitchen with her sister following. Kevin set Ricky down and asked him to help his mother, then motioned for Alex to join him outside. Alex set the cast-iron skillet on the counter, then followed Kevin.

The door closed behind them, and Alex spoke before his younger brother could say a word. "I did mean a few extra days, Kevin. Something came up while I was there that threw a monkey wrench into my plans.''

''And in two weeks you couldn't find time to call?'' Kevin took a deep breath and stared him in the eye.

''I was on a couple of fires.''

''I can't have a foreman who disappears in the middle of a contract, Alex. We've been through this before. If you want to fight fires, that's great. I know you love it.'' He paused, crossing his arms over his chest. ''Things have taken off, and I could definitely use an experienced hand. However, I'll find someone else if you don't want to fill in. But when I need you, I need you here. Maybe it's better this happened right off the bat.''

Alex wished there were a way to explain the sudden changes he'd been through in the past month. Now wasn't the time. There was no way he was going to admit to Kevin the problem was that Alex thought he'd fallen in love with Katarina. Next thing he knew, Kevin would tell his wife, and then Emily would tell Katarina. Then she'd bolt like lightning back to that ''almost fiancé'' of hers. ''I'm in. Don't worry, Kevin. I'm through fighting fires. It's time I settle down.''

Kevin quirked his eyebrow. ''Settle down?'' A sudden smile spread across his brother's face. ''This—'' he made an all-encompassing gesture with his hands ''—is all about a woman? Why didn't you just say so?''

All of a sudden, Alex realized what Kevin was thinking—that there was someone back in Montana that he'd been working things out with.

Alex shook his head. "You have this all wrong."

Kevin slapped him jovially on the shoulder. "I guess you do have a few things to fill me in on, bro. Another MacIntyre brother breaks the pact." The front door opened and Emily called them for dinner.

Alex felt the tension in the room when they entered. "I didn't mean to barge in on anything. I'll just leave you all to enjoy your evening. I'd better be finding a place to stay." He picked up his bags and headed back out the door, before Kevin changed his mind about being mad over his late arrival. The last thing he needed tonight was to put his foot in his mouth again.

"You can't leave now." Emily stopped him. "Join us for supper. We can settle living arrangements while we eat."

Kevin looked at him, then Katarina. "We haven't had a chance to move my stuff completely out, so Katarina's things are mostly on the main floor. If you don't mind my junk, Alex, you can use the upstairs for now. You and Kat could share the kitchen and living room." Everyone moved to the table except Alex.

"There's plenty of room for both of you. After all, you're practically family. And neither of you is really ready to sign a lease or commit to a long-term arrangement,'' Emily added. ''This will buy you both some time to get settled.''

Had his brother and sister-in-law really suggested he share the house with Katarina? Were they totally blind? Or maybe he was the only one who could see the obvious, that he was crazy to even entertain the thought of him and Katarina together.

''We had this same argument with Kat,'' Emily pointed out. ''It's silly to waste all this space.''

They were right—there was more than enough room in the seventies-style passive solar home. The loft upstairs consisted of a spacious master suite, an oversize bath and a den that overlooked the living area below.

On the main floor, the great room was the central hub, flanked on one side by the kitchen, formal dining area and a breakfast nook, and on the other side by two bedrooms and a bathroom. The utility room also served as a mudroom, connecting the garage to the kitchen.

It might work temporarily. ''Well,'' Alex said, still thinking. He took a deep breath. *A man could get used to this life pretty easy, Lord. If it's not meant to be, I'd just as soon hightail it out of here now, before anyone gets hurt.*

Katarina was silent. Had been since he arrived. It seemed obvious that she didn't like the idea. As if she could read his mind, she interrupted his thoughts. ''There's plenty of Stroganoff left from Ron's visit, Alex. Have a seat and help yourself.''

Their eyes met. She smiled, revealing none of her previous annoyance. Had he simply surprised her with his arrival? Or was she truly not bothered by Kevin and Emily's suggestion? "If you're sure you don't mind."

"Of course not."

"Good, I'm glad that's settled," Kevin declared.

The comment could be taken several different ways, Alex realized when Katarina looked at him in shock. They obviously had a few more things to discuss on the housing issue. At least he had Emily and Kevin convinced that it was a done deal.

"Dinner smells great," Alex offered as they sat down. The conversation moved toward each of their respective lives, with no mention of Katarina's job. When the room became suddenly silent, Alex realized they were waiting for him to fill them in on what he'd been doing for the past two weeks.

He hesitated. "Since I missed the refresher course this spring, I went ahead with that, just in case."

"Just in case?" Kevin echoed. "In case what? I thought we just cleared that up. You said you're done fighting fires. I hope to keep you busy enough to give that up altogether."

"You know Alex, a real Boy Scout—he's always prepared for any emergency." Katarina laughed at her repeat of the insult he'd thrown at Ron.

Alex laughed, hoping her jab was enough to end Kevin's questions. "You have to admit, my planning paid off."

Katarina's blue eyes brimmed with laughter. "That's a matter of opinion."

"And how did your interview go?" Alex took a bite of rice and followed it with a strip of beef.

"Just say 'I told you so' and get it over with."

Alex looked around the table, each looking at their dinner. "What happened?"

"You blew her big chance," Ricky proclaimed.

All eyes turned to the little boy as his mother shushed him.

"It was just like you said—it wasn't in God's plan, I guess," Katarina corrected.

Alex looked at her, wishing everything about that trip had gone differently. "I'm sure another window will open, Katarina."

Emily set her fork down. "Of course it will."

"Until then, I've a backlog of orders to keep me busy. Another boutique signed a contract for a monthly shipment. I'm taking applicants for an assistant, by the way. If anyone knows of a good seamstress..." Katarina pushed her chair away from the table. "Would anyone like some strawberry shortcake?"

The evening came to an early close after the dishes were done. "I'll see you at the office, first thing in the morning?" Kevin added as he walked out of the house.

"I'll be there." Alex closed the door behind them and looked again at his bags. "I'm not sure this is the best plan, Katarina. Maybe I should find a hotel until I can get an apartment.''

Katarina backed away and leaned against the stair railing. She stuffed her hands into her shorts pockets. ''Why did you come back?''

What did he dare say? *Because I think I love you* seemed a bit premature. ''Two weeks ago you asked me what gave me any right to preach to you about God's will. I was going to turn Kevin down—keep on fighting fires—but I couldn't. I kept getting this feeling I was needed here, for what exact purpose I have yet to figure out. Who am I to question God?''

His comment seemed to amuse her. ''You could have saved yourself the effort,'' she said defensively.

He smiled in return. ''And why's that?''

She defiantly tucked a lock of that honey-blond hair behind her ear. ''Because I can take care of myself. And that includes my faith.''

Alex wanted nothing more than to point out the error of her thinking, but bit his tongue. He had to leave that in God's hands. ''Then I guess that answers one question, doesn't it?''

Katarina crossed her arms over her breast. ''What's that?''

''Silly me, I wondered if He had in mind to bring me back here for you. Thanks for clearing that up.'' Alex picked up his bags and headed toward the stairs to the loft, catching the look on her face.

Katarina's smile faltered as he brushed past her.

"I'm glad we've made that perfectly clear." Her gaze locked with his momentarily, the fire still simmering between them.

Who does she think she's kidding?

"This is a temporary situation," he assured her.

"Of course it is. I'll be glad to keep my things in the two bedrooms down here, if you'll please offer the same for the upstairs. We do our own laundry. Fix our own meals, wash our own dishes..."

It appeared Katarina actually believed this could work. Didn't she have a clue what he was feeling for her? "I wouldn't consider anything less than sharing the housework, fifty-fifty."

"If you'll show me how to run the mower, I'll be glad to help with the lawn work."

He stared at her. "Sure. I'd be glad to. You're positive you don't mind me bunking here?"

She shrugged. "Why should I mind? You're my brother-in-law's brother. We're practically related. Oh, one more thing, no more sneaking into the house and scaring me half to death."

"Sorry about that. If I'd known you were staying here, I'd have called first." *So, today I'm a brother. I guess it beats being her father. Is this considered progress, God?*

The tone of Katarina's voice stopped his prayer short. "It's not like there could ever be anything between *us*, right?"

God, help me out here. Katarina is one fire I

haven't a clue how to douse. I tried walking away, and You told me to come back. Someone has mountains to move here, and I hope You don't think I'm going to do it alone!

Chapter Thirteen

Katarina disappeared into the garage to pour slip into the doll molds and fire a batch of porcelain arms and legs. An hour later, she went out to the gazebo to enjoy the fresh air and try to push thoughts of Alex from her mind. *Who am I trying to kid? Even a thousand miles didn't help.* Even when he was in Montana, Katarina had found herself thinking of him, wondering what he was doing and if their disastrous trip had anything to do with him staying away.

Getting Alex off her mind was going to be impossible with him sharing the house. Why didn't she just tell him she didn't want him here? *Because it's his brother's house. If anyone should leave, it's me.*

She'd just paid the deductible on the car insurance, sent out another mailing for Kat's Kreations with a second change of address in as many months, and rented a box at the post office so she wouldn't have to go through all of this again. No, her leaving was out of the question. She'd just have to make the best of the situation. After all, it was only temporary. Sharing a house didn't oblige her to become best of friends.

How was she ever going to explain this to Ron? Or would he even care, for that matter? He hadn't been bothered by her traveling with Alex, simply annoyed that she had kept him waiting all night for her phone call.

Katarina closed her eyes. Was Emily right? Did she unconsciously hold others at an arm's distance to protect herself? How could she ever trust anyone with her heart again when the one man she'd thought she could trust above all others had walked away? Would memories of her father's leaving ever stop tormenting her?

Katarina recalled her earlier conversation with Alex, and his claim that God had brought him back to Springville. She'd felt a momentary spark of hope, despite the warnings her mind kept sending her heart. *What did you expect, Kat, him to fall on one knee and proclaim his undying love? Not a chance.* Katarina set the swing in motion again, watching threads of clouds drift past the full moon. *Keep playing it safe, Katarina. Stick with Ron. Sometimes boring and predictable are best.*

Inside, a small voice affirmed Emily's observation. Keeping people at arm's length was the only way she knew to keep from getting hurt. She'd let James break through the wall to her heart, and he'd betrayed her. She blinked back tears, despising how weak they made her feel. Tears that reminded her of the day her daddy left. That rekindled her feelings of worthlessness, loneliness and fear.

"Katarina." A door inside the house closed, then another, and Alex called her name again.

If You're listening, God, I beg You to get Alex out of this house. The porch light went on, and he repeated her name. Katarina pulled the hearing aid from her ear so she couldn't hear him and closed her eyes as if doing so would hide her from Alex. She held still, hoping not to draw his attention.

A few minutes later, he was right there with her. The surprise on his face was genuine. "Hi. I guess you didn't hear me calling. I gave up looking for you and decided I'd come sit in the 'zebro' for a bit." Alex smiled. "I didn't realize you were out here. Do you mind if I join you?"

Very funny, God. I meant out of the house for good, not out here, now. Despite Alex's naturally loud voice, it was still awkward trying to carry on a conversation. Katarina felt the hearing aid in her hand. "No, I…I took my hearing aid out. Did you need something?"

He sat down on the step and looked at her, raising his voice. "I need to unload the truck, and noticed some things in the garage. I thought I'd better see if there is a specific place you'd like me to put my tools.''

Katarina took a step to the arched entrance, and Alex stood, letting her pass. That usual spark of attraction ignited within her. She immediately extinguished it and headed for the house.

Alex said something, but it was all garbled.

Brilliant idea taking your hearing aid out, Kat. Now how do you expect to carry on a semicoherent conversation with the man? And you can't exactly put it back in now without explaining why you took it out in the first place.

Katarina stopped and turned her better ear to Alex. "I missed that. What did you say?"

He stepped far closer than necessary and gently repeated his question. She felt the warmth of his breath on her neck. "I didn't notice a car anywhere. What's going on with the insurance?"

"It hasn't been settled yet." Katarina raised her gaze to meet his and felt her breathing quicken. She fingered her hearing aid, wishing this obsession to avoid Alex would stop getting her into trouble. "Let me go get my hearing aid back in, and I'll meet you in the garage."

A few minutes later, she went out there, half in anticipation, half in dread. She read the gauge on the kiln, opened a peephole and turned to Alex.

"Now, what were we talking about?" Katarina asked, hopefully masking her inner turmoil with a deceptive calmness. Katarina carefully removed the molds from the doll heads she'd poured after supper.

"You've been without a car for nearly two weeks?"

She nodded casually. As Alex talked, she cut holes into the heads for the teeth and eyes, and set them on the shelf to finish drying so she could fire them in the morning. He stared at her, his blue eyes sharp and keenly observing her every move.

Alex's voice was soft, as if the sound would break the greenware. "What's that divot for?"

"Dimples, silly."

His eyebrows shot up. "Hmmm. Amazing. So, why'd you return the rental?" Alex lowered his gaze and his voice. "I told you to keep it as long as it took to replace your car, Kat."

"I've managed just fine. There was no need to run up a huge bill. Besides, it's been good incentive to stay home and get back on schedule. I've almost caught up with my orders after the move."

Alex studied her face with his tender gaze and Kat realized she had to conquer her involuntary reaction to that gentle, loving look of his. "Be careful, Katarina, working overtime is habit-forming. I thought you were going to hire some help."

"I have two interviews lined up for tomorrow."

Without lingering on his advice, or arguing about her not keeping the rental car, Alex proceeded to ask where he could set his equipment without it being in her way.

The two worked side by side late into the evening. When they'd finished, Alex looked at his watch. "It's nearly ten already. If there's an ice cream place still open, I'd like to take you for dessert."

Surprised by his suggestion, Katarina wondered if he knew she loved ice cream. "Sure, I found a great little parlor on my way to the grocery store the other day. It's just a few blocks away. I think they close at ten-thirty. If we hurry, we can make it."

Alex closed the garage door and went into the house. "It would be a nice night for a walk. If there's time."

"It would," she said softly, afraid to let herself enjoy Alex's company. Katarina pocketed her keys and joined him at the front door.

Because there were so many cars lining the narrow streets, they crowded onto the sidewalk next to each other, falling into a synchronized gait. Katarina felt her heart beat faster with each step she took. "So you went back to fight fires, huh?"

"It only took a couple to decide it's time I moved on."

"I thought that was your plan when you went to Montana…to come back here, I mean." She stopped, her feet suddenly anchored to the sidewalk. "I feel responsible for…"

Alex looked surprised. Then amused. "Responsible for what?" He stared at her with a warm intensity, waiting.

She blinked. "I don't know really, for—" Katarina shrugged, then laughed nervously "—scaring you out of coming back, I guess. I don't know. I'm sorry...forget I said anything." What was she thinking? Alex had done nothing to imply he had a personal interest in her.

Without answering, he touched her arm and started them walking again. "We don't want to miss our ice cream."

A light breeze cooled the evening and filled the air with the pungent aroma of a flower garden. A block had passed and Alex hadn't spoken. Katarina was even more embarrassed that she'd said anything.

"For the record, God and I had a few things to work out before I could come back."

"Oh, that's a relief." It wasn't a relief at all, as now she felt even more ridiculous for thinking he'd stayed away because of her. "Turn left here." She motioned, accidentally brushing her arm against his.

He pivoted and rested his hand on her back while the traffic cleared, then let it drop to his side when they'd crossed the street. Finally they made it to the front of the line in the crowded ice cream parlor.

Alex waited while she ordered a dip of chocolate chip mint on a waffle cone. "I'll have one scoop of bubble gum, and a dip of Rocky Road—in memory of our road trip."

Katarina cringed as she laughed. "Rocky Road and bubble gum?"

"Yeah," he drawled. "Keeps life interesting."

She pulled a ten-dollar bill from her pocket.

Alex covered her hand with his. "It's my treat. That was a delicious dinner."

"It was just leftovers."

He raised one eyebrow. "Must have been a pretty special dinner the first time around, then."

She licked her ice cream and smiled. "You probably don't want to hear about it."

Alex pocketed his change and took a bite of the Rocky Road. "Probably not. Next week I'll fix dinner, and you can spring for dessert."

Alex tiptoed around the kitchen the next morning so as not to wake Katarina. Anxious to start back to work, he settled for a bowl of cereal and a glass of juice. After an unsuccessful search for a coffeepot, Alex decided to get a cup of java on the way to the office. Since he hadn't taken time to stop at the market the night before, he'd have to grab a quick lunch today.

Knowing he'd be home at six was a luxury he'd almost forgotten. Two fires, and it was no longer something to be taken for granted. He stepped into the garage, surprised to find Katarina already working. "You been out here all night?"

"Off and on," she said without looking up.

He studied her organized mess. "Is my truck in your way? I'll be glad to leave it in the driveway, if it is."

Katarina pasted a smile on her lips. "I've managed to keep from getting any additional 'mud' on it.''

He laughed, looking at the splattered truck. ''You making fun of my truck?''

Kat didn't say a word, just kept scraping the doll arm. She moved it closer. Alex leaned forward to see what she was concentrating so intently on. Her blue eyes narrowed behind the protective glasses, and her tongue poked out from the corner of her mouth.

Alex sent up a quick prayer of patience, reminding himself that he was here for Kevin and his own future. If he won Katarina's heart in the process, all that much better. *Who am I kidding? All I ask, God, is that You protect both of us if this isn't meant to be.* He waited until she looked up again.

Katarina smiled. ''Sorry, I didn't realize you were talking to me.''

''I didn't want to startle you and make you drop what you were working on. I'm surprised to see you up already.''

''I couldn't sleep last night, and decided I may as well get some work done.''

He stepped over to his truck. ''I'm going to the store on my way home tonight. Do you need anything?''

Her expression brightened, then she squashed it, as if unwilling to accept his help. ''No, I'm fine.''

He shook his head. She was one stubborn woman.

"You need some way to get around and it is my fault you're without a car."

"I'm managing, but thank you for the offer."

"I see." Determined. Independent. And he admired her far more for both.

She kept her feelings in tight control. "Have a good day, Alex."

"I'll see you tonight," he said lightly. He got into his truck and opened the electric garage door.

"I'll be here," she mumbled.

"On the other hand, I think I'll come home and clean up before I go to the store. I forget, I'm not thirty miles from nowhere anymore. If you'd like to ride along, that'd be fine." He started the engine and backed out, letting her have the day to think about the suggestion.

On the way, Alex made a quick stop at the convenience store to fill the tank with gas and get a cup of coffee. Kevin glanced up from the desk when Alex walked in. "Morning, stranger."

"Morning. How's the medical clinic coming along? Almost done?" He'd enjoyed working on the project and looked forward to seeing the crew again.

Kevin clicked on the print icon and folded his hands behind his head. "Final walk-through today. Why don't you come along, see what you think? Then we have an interesting project to discuss."

By noon they'd completed the walk-through and made assignments on the touch-ups, then stopped for lunch. "Did you ever take that seminar on log homes?"

Alex nodded. "I even bought the land, just never got around to building. Helped Greg with his in our spare time. Haven't had another winter mild enough to get mine done."

"Adam is going to build onto the ranch. Wants log and river rock, to blend in with Grandma and Grandpa's home. He has an outlandish bid from some company out of Aspen, and asked if we'd like to give it a shot. He has the building permit approved and has a plan picked out. The kit could be there next week. What do you think?"

Alex looked his brother in the eye. "You're the boss. Is that something you want to tackle?"

"Combine some family time with work. Sounds like more fun than work."

"What about Emily's schedule and Ricky? You sure you want to be away so much?" Alex took a bite of enchilada. They discussed the other bids they wanted to take on. Helping their youngest brother won hands down. "I don't want to see you putting work before your family."

Kevin smiled. "I appreciate that. I was actually wondering if you'd like to take the lead on this one? I could juggle the projects here."

Alex felt a smile spread from ear to ear. "I'd love to. When do you want to start?"

"You want to go out and take a look now?"

Alex jumped from his seat and grabbed the bill.

The drive to Loveland took a little over an hour, which made it even more appealing to stay with Adam and get the job done as quickly as possible. He wondered if that was why Kevin and Emily had suggested he and Katarina share the house in the first place, knowing Alex would be out of town a lot.

After Adam told them the plans he had for his dude ranch, they went over the blueprints and possible time line for the project. Alex jotted down notes to use in the figuring of a bid. The three stopped at their mother's house on the north side of the creek for a glass of tea and some of her famous molasses cookies before Alex and Kevin headed home.

On the way, Kevin brought up the conversation Alex had hoped would take a long time to resurface. "What's this about you settling down? Who's the lucky woman?"

"I didn't say a thing about a woman."

"You didn't have to. There was that sparkle in your eye. I...wouldn't happen to know her, would I?"

Alex shook his head. "Don't put the cart before the horse, Kevin. There are a few mountains to move before I could even venture a guess on that one."

"She's stubborn, huh?"

Alex chuckled. "You could say that," he admitted before catching his slip.

Kevin had a mischievous grin on his face. "It runs in the family."

"Is it that obvious?"

Kevin laughed. "Well, if Kat hadn't come home from your trip ready to spit nails, it *might* have slipped past us." His brother tapped his fingers on the steering wheel, then shook his head. "Nah, I take it back. I think the wedding was when I figured it out."

"And Emily?"

"I had her figured out long before that," Kevin said with another chuckle.

"I mean, what does she think about it?"

"We both decided that's between the two of you."

Alex laughed. "That's the biggest cop-out I've ever heard."

"It's my story, and I'm sticking to it."

Chapter Fourteen

Katarina closed her eyes and silently fumbled with the words that were tearing her apart. Words too painful to say out loud. How could she forgive the man who had walked out on his responsibility? How could she let go of the pain? The anger? *I don't know what to do, God. I don't know if I can do this alone. Emily's busy with her job and new family. Lisa's hardly even accessible by phone anymore. And Mom doesn't understand. She's never had time to listen to me. Ron listens, but…I may as well be talking to a wall. I want to believe that You're hearing me. And once in a while, I think You've answered my prayers, but then I find a way to reason it out to circumstances, to coincidence.*

She woke in the night, burdened by the feelings she had for her father. She'd stretched and tied Emily's advice into knots for the past week. Yet no matter how she tried to contort His word, the truth always snapped back at her like elastic. "God will not leave you," Emily had told her. "You are His precious child."

I want to believe that, God. I want to understand. Let me open my heart to others. Teach me to trust.

"I'll be glad to do this, Katarina." Alex took a step toward the lawn mower.

She jerked the cord again. Nothing happened. "There must be something wrong with it. You sure there isn't one of those key thingies somewhere?"

"Sorry, my brother's a little less extravagant, I guess. Here, let me show you." Alex stood behind Katarina and placed his hand over hers. He wrapped her fingers firmly around the handle of the pull cord and yanked.

The mower started right up. "Now if you press this lever..." He looked at Katarina, who was pointing to the ear protector in her good ear, indicating she couldn't hear him. Taking hold of the handle, Alex pushed the lever forward and engaged the power drive. It pulled both of them across the middle of the yard. When she reached the first corner, he showed her how to lift the front drive wheels off the ground and make the turn, then he let her go on her own while he edged the lawn.

Alex felt they had made decent progress in the past week. She was no longer hiding out in the gazebo or finding excuses to be occupied when he

came home from work. Until today, he'd success-
fully maintained a comfortable and "safe" distance
between them. Even that hadn't stopped sparks from
flying. And tonight he felt as if lightning was about
to strike. He'd come home after work to find her
dressed in grubby jeans and a pretty pink tank top,
ready for her lesson on how to run the mower.

The motor died, and Alex looked up.

"Why is it dropping clumps of grass everywhere?
Did I break it?"

He smiled warmly and shook his head, then
stepped close so she could hear him. "Nothing's
wrong. It just means the grass catcher is full." It
took him five minutes to figure out how to detach
the catcher. She held the bag, then insisted on con-
tinuing with the job herself. She managed to get it
started after a couple of tries. Before she could argue, he carried the bags of clippings to the curb.

By the time Alex finished the edging, cleaned the
equipment and put everything away, Katarina was
grilling teriyaki chicken for the two of them. "I
thought we had an agreement about meals."

Katarina had changed into shorts and a T-shirt.
"The recipe makes far too much for just me. I
thought it might be nice to simplify things for one
night, since you were kind enough to help me with
the yard. It took much longer than I expected."

Alex felt his willpower slipping away with her
sudden change of heart. "The grass was pretty long.

If one of us mows every week, it shouldn't be so bad. Do you mind if I go clean up?''

Katarina shrugged. ''Go ahead. This'll take a while.''

Alex returned downstairs as Katarina started setting the table. ''Why don't we sit outside. Enjoy the hard work you put into the yard before this storm moves in on us.''

Katarina served up her plate and handed him an empty one to serve himself. ''What would you like to drink?'' The rasp in her voice hadn't been there earlier, and he wondered if it was a reaction to the dust from the mower, or intentional.

He wiped the cool perspiration from his brow and forced his mind back to the food. ''I'd have lemonade if it's made. If not, water.''

Katarina poured them both glasses of lemonade and carried them outside to the porch. They lingered over dinner, as if neither were as hungry for nourishment as they were for each other's company. They moved to the swing in the gazebo to watch the sun being chased out by the electrical storm. A few minutes later the landscape lights turned on, giving the yard a gentle glow.

''How is your seamstress working out?''

''Great, you'll have to meet her. I can't believe how much more I'm able to accomplish this way. I love her work, and that frees me up to concentrate on the dolls.''

''That's great. Have you always worked alone?''

Katarina pulled her knees to her chest and Alex kept the swing moving. "In college a few friends helped, but they weren't as conscientious as I wanted. I decided it was better to do it myself."

"I'm glad you're learning to let someone else take a little of your load. You can't do it all yourself."

She lifted her chin defiantly. "I've done okay so far."

"I didn't mean it as an insult." He rested his hand on her shoulder and moved closer. "I wish you weren't so defensive. I meant that as a positive. You want your company to grow, and that takes delegation."

"Then why didn't you say that in the first place?"

He shrugged. "Guess I need to work on communicating with a woman…and maybe you could accept that not all men are out to hurt you."

She hugged her legs tighter and rested her chin on her bare knees. "I'm sorry, it's a natural instinct for me."

"I've noticed." Alex rubbed the soft skin on her neck and struggled with whether to take the conversation to the next level. "I don't want to hurt you, Katarina. So if it happens, know that it's never intentional."

He knew the pain of losing a father, but he couldn't imagine how much it hurt knowing her father had chosen to abandon his family. As if that wasn't painful enough, Katarina had to live with this constant reminder of her father's actions. What kind of man could do this to a child?

Alex fought the urge to wrap her in his arms and tell Katarina what a wonderful child her father had created and how angry it made him that the man had caused her such pain.

"May I ask you something, Alex?"

"Of course. What is it?" He searched her face, reaching into her thoughts, offering silent comfort and support to the one woman he longed to love.

"How do you know what God's will for you is?"

He sucked in a long breath. The answer seemed so simple to one who knew and trusted the heavenly Father. Yet, to Katarina, nothing was simple. Fathers didn't stick around. Fathers weren't to be trusted, and she'd made it perfectly clear she didn't need another. "I asked God to show me what He wanted me to do with my life. For years, that was fighting fires."

Katarina's gaze was fixed on him, her eyes betraying the fear inside.

Father, help me to say the right thing. "Last year, after my accident, I had to sit out the last fire. I lost two close friends and struggled with going back ever since."

"Is that why you went back? To face your fear?"

Alex shook his head. "I thought I was afraid for a while, but finally realized that wasn't it. I still love fighting fires, but this time the drive wasn't there. It wasn't enough." He leaned forward and rested his elbows on his knees. "There was something missing. God and I had quite a few discussions about the matter. I didn't want to think of life without jumping. Coming back here, I found the missing link—family."

She looked even more puzzled. "I'm sure this sounds very elementary, but how do you know He's talking to you?"

"Some people very clearly 'hear' a voice. I asked Him to help me to put my own desires aside, to take them away if they weren't in His plan. As much as I tried to deny His answer, that longing to come back here didn't go away, and my 'spark' for fighting fires went out."

"Do you miss it now that you're here?"

He hated to see Katarina hurting. "Sure I do, sometimes. But not the way you might think. I'm very much at peace with the decision. I miss the jumps, the beauty, the people. I don't miss it as much as I enjoy being here." A long silence stretched between them, and Alex waited, hoping she would say more. "Katarina, God is willing to take your burdens, if you ask Him."

"That's what's so confusing. I've done that. And it doesn't seem like He hears me. Maybe I'm asking for the wrong thing. I don't understand."

"He knows your needs. He knows the plans He has for you and your future."

"I thought it was to sell my designs, but that obviously wasn't it. Now I don't know what He has in store. Ron keeps pushing in one direction, and that makes sense, but it's not working out at all according to our plans.''

Alex felt a slight twinge of guilt that their plans weren't going well, but it went away quickly. As long as she and Ron were out of sorts, there was hope. *Your will, Father, not mine.* "I hope hiring help means you'll be able to take a little more time to relax.''

"This from a man who spent days on end fighting fires without sleep? And who's going to be staying on his next job site in order to put in more hours?'' she teased.

Alex placed his hand on the seat behind her and leaned close. "If you object, I can always change my plans.''

Katarina's blue eyes met his, and the subtle look of amusement faded away. Her demure smile invited him to toss aside his principles and give her a kiss that would make her forget the Boy Scout.

"Tell me that 'fiancé' of yours is out of the picture, Katarina, and I'll be the first to congratulate you. In the meantime, I won't add to your confusion.''

His words didn't register on her dizzied senses until he stood up and pulled her to her feet.

"True love has no doubts. True love casts away fear. Listen to your heart. I think you know what it is that God's trying to tell you. You draw that line, Kat, and I'll respect it.''

Katarina felt like a fool. She wanted Alex to kiss her, to let his strong embrace comfort her and let her feel special, if only for a few minutes.

"Go on inside, Alex. Please. I want to be alone." She turned her back to him and stared into the stormy sky.

Alex rested his hands on her shoulders. "You're never alone, Kat. Our heavenly Father is always with you." His comforting words were a warm blanket around her. And then he left.

She leaned against the post and let the breeze cool her. Lightning crackled and sliced the sky, and turned the darkness into a spectacular light show. Katarina looked at Alex. The shadow of his lean, rugged body filled the patio door.

Raindrops pelted the gazebo, splatting against the lattice walls in a squall that lasted less than five minutes and did little more than tease regarding the much-needed moisture. She brushed the mist from her face and noted Alex was still there. Was he watching the storm? Or her?

Oh, Alex, where were you when Ron came along?

Chapter Fifteen

"Come on, Kat, we want you to come. It's Kevin's birthday," Emily begged.

"You won't miss me." Katarina was thankful that she didn't have to face Alex that next morning. He'd already left for Adam's when she awoke. She wondered idly what he had been thinking since she'd asked him to leave the gazebo. She'd been sure he was going to kiss her. And her embarrassment refused to go away.

Emily continued chopping vegetables. "We will, too. And you've been looking forward to camping. Come on. What's wrong? Did something happen between you and Alex?"

You read minds now, Dr. Emily? "No, nothing happened."

"Then what is it?" Emily's voice took on that all-knowing-big-sister tone.

Katarina laughed sarcastically. "Don't you dare get that tone with me."

Emily smiled. "Sparks are flying, aren't they? Surely I don't need to tell you, the 'heart specialist,' that Alex is a wonderful guy."

"Yeah, a real Boy Scout."

Emily nudged Katarina with her hip. "Come on, tell me what's going on."

She turned serious. "I did tell you. Nothing." Kat hesitated, feeling her face flush all over again at her sister's stare of disbelief. "Okay. I thought he was going to kiss me, and he backed away at the last minute, because of Ron."

"Really? That's...nice of him." Emily said, clearly as puzzled as Katarina. "I mean, chivalrous, I guess."

"It was for the best. Now you see why I don't want to go. I mean, I'm the one who is supposedly committed to Ron, and I wanted Alex to kiss me."

"You're not even sure you want to stay with Ron, are you?"

Silence.

"Be honest, Kat. You're having doubts, aren't you?"

True love has no doubts. Katarina shook her head. *If that's true, Alex, I couldn't truly love you, either.* "We've been together for nearly two years. It's..."

"A safety net. That's all. Ron and you share none of the passion, for anything, that sustains a marriage. He's convenient. He doesn't challenge your comfort zone. He doesn't enjoy any of the things you do.

Kat, you wouldn't be happy with him. Tell me, did you have a wonderful time when he came to visit?"

"Passion wasn't enough for Dad, either."

Emily looked out the window again, checking on Ricky in his new sandbox. "Don't try to figure out what went wrong for Mom and Dad. We only know Mom's side of the story—which is very biased. You can't live in the past."

"Those who forget the past are destined to repeat it."

Emmy held up her hands in defeat. "Don't live in fear of repeating it. Change history, Katarina. Do you even love Ron?"

The words wouldn't come from Katarina's mouth. She took a drink of water and looked at Emily. "I thought so."

"Until?"

"I met Alex." Emily said nothing. "And it scares me." Katarina gathered the chocolate chip cookies from the cooling rack and put them in a bag. "Alex has just left a career that he loved so much that he stayed single in order to continue the job. I know he's very happy working with Kevin, too, Em, but...I shouldn't have said anything."

"All I'm hearing is fear, Kat. And pretty lousy reasons not to take a chance on someone you care for, I might add. What is it that attracts you to him?"

Katarina leaned her head back on the sofa and closed her eyes. "He's so thoughtful, and friendly, protective." The words flowed easily. "He's analytical, and open, funny, energetic and strong—not just physically, but emotionally and spiritually. He's so easy to talk to." Katarina opened her eyes. "Now I sound like that lovesick eighteen-year-old again."

Emily laughed softly. "Not quite. When you were eighteen all you noticed was that he was a hunk. You didn't even mention that today."

Katarina blushed. "Well, that goes without saying."

"So what's the worst thing that could happen, Kat?"

They both knew the answer to that one.

Without saying another word, Emily started carrying the gear to the Suburban. "Come help, then we'll go get your things packed. I'm not leaving you home alone on the Fourth of July."

When they arrived at Whispering Pines Ranch two hours later, Alex, Kevin and Adam were waiting to unload the food and sleeping bags. Six tents littered what looked like a pasture with split rail fences surrounding it. Beyond the next fence, horses whinnied. Behind the house were some sort of camp stove and tables under a green-and-white-striped awning.

Kevin and Emily greeted each other warmly. "Come on, you two, it's only been two days since you've been apart," Adam interrupted. "Love, it's pathetic." He winked at Katarina. "Let me show you where to set that." She followed the youngest MacIntyre into the old house.

Avoiding Alex was easy, thanks to Ricky. The

little boy had obviously found his own hero. Adam carried the coolers to the kitchen and helped Katarina move the perishables into the refrigerator while Kevin helped Emily ''situate'' their tent. Alex took Ricky to check out the guys' tent.

Mrs. MacIntyre came into the kitchen while Adam went for the next load. ''It's so good to have you join us, Katarina. I wish your younger sister could have come.''

Kat smiled at Alex's mother. ''I'm sure Lisa would love it here. She's always searching for a beautiful focal point for her camera. Whispering Pines fits that bill.''

''Poor Adam fell in love with this place as a boy. He had no idea he'd be stuck with me, too.''

Alex and Ricky appeared, each carrying grocery sacks. ''Yeah, poor, poor, Adam. He's stuck, all right. Trying to keep up with his mother is tough on the kid.''

Millie smiled as Alex wrapped his arm around his mother's shoulders. She jabbed him in the ribs. ''I didn't see you passing me up yesterday.''

Adam walked through the door, laughing. ''Yeah, bro. You ought to talk!''

''Hey, it's not my fault you gave me old Gertrude. I could have beat the both of you if I'd had your mount.''

Alex looked happier than she'd ever seen him. He looked at Katarina, his blue eyes piercing the distance between them. ''Come on up to the pasture, and I'll show you to your palace, ma'am. It has a bit different accommodations than our last camp-out, as I recall.''

Katarina sucked in a breath. She hoped that coming here wasn't a huge mistake.

Ricky started to tag along, but Adam caught his attention. ''Why don't Grandma and I show you our horses?''

''Real horses?'' The three headed straight across the pasture, and Alex led her to the right.

Katarina looked accusingly at Alex. ''Why, the little traitor. Bought off by a measly horse.''

Alex laughed, and Katarina joined him.

''Let's grab your bags. I trust you packed warmer clothes this trip.''

''Yours were so cozy, I thought I'd just use them. I was sure you wouldn't mind,'' she retorted.

''I'll have to remember that in the future, in case any of my clothes come up missing.'' A smile teased his lips and he took her overloaded suitcase from the back of the Suburban and groaned. ''I see you didn't want to take any chances this time.''

''Nope.''

Alex motioned toward the gate and followed her through. ''Third tent on the right. You'll notice I've gone to great lengths to make sure your first camping experience is a pleasant one.''

For an instant she forgot the embarrassment of the other night. ''It was...quite memorable. And in case you've forgotten, this is my second camp-out.''

''Then I hope I can make your second just as memorable as the first.'' Katarina noticed the warm smile hiding behind his tense jaw. "I believe I agreed to show you what camping is supposed to be like." He stopped by a blue-and-maroon tent, unzipped the opening and set her bag inside. "The finest tent available, just for you."

Katarina looked at him suspiciously as she stepped into the domed shelter. "There's only one problem, Mr. Bellhop." Katarina placed her hands on her hips and spun around to face him.

Alex quirked his eyebrows. "Yes?"

"We're *not* sharing a tent."

"But we share a house," he countered.

Katarina stepped back and pointed at the two sleeping bags. "A house. A *huge* house, not a…tiny room," she said, lowering her voice to a grumble.

Alex shrugged. "I didn't make the sleeping assignments, sorry." His lip twitched. "Katarina…"

She took another step backward and tumbled over her suitcase and onto the tent floor. "Ouch!" Katarina paused. "You can get out, and take your sleeping bag with you." She picked up the pillow and threw it at him.

Alex hopped out of the way, caught the pillow and peeked his head back inside. "Have it your way, Kat, but it's not my sleeping bag."

"Then whose is it?"

"Alex, is there a problem?" Mrs. MacIntyre's shadow rounded the tent before she did.

"No problem, Mother. Just trying to settle your roomie's nerves."

Katarina felt the blush crawl clear to her neck. She covered her face with her hands.

"Oh," Alex said, leaning back inside, "here."

Katarina looked up just as the pillow smacked her in the face. *His mother? How many more ways can I make a fool of myself in front of this family?* She collapsed back onto the sleeping bag and covered her face with the pillow.

Mrs. MacIntyre stepped inside. "Are you okay, Katarina?"

"Fine, I'm just fine."

"You'll have to excuse the boys, dear. They've had such fun setting things up for this party. We've so enjoyed having Alex here the past few days."

Katarina groaned quietly, hoping the pillow muffled the sound from Mrs. MacIntyre's ears.

"I do hope you don't mind me sharing your tent. The boys thought I should stay in the house, but they seem to have forgotten who taught them how to camp."

Kat pulled the pillow from her face and sat up. "I don't mind at all, Mrs. Mac…"

"Call me Millie, please."

Alex popped his head back into the tent. The smoldering flame she saw in his gaze startled her. "You ready for a riding lesson?"

Katarina looked at Millie, then Alex. "Riding what?"

"Horses."

"Really? You're not teasing me again, are you?"

"Cross my heart."

She smiled. "Okay. As long as I get dear, sweet old Gertrude."

He offered Katarina a hand and led her past his mother. "You want to join us, Mom?"

"I'll stay with Ricky and wait for the others to arrive." The three walked toward the barn.

"Adam's taking him. We'll fix the burgers later." Alex glanced at his watch. "The others won't be here for at least an hour. Why don't you go ahead and put your feet up for a while?"

Millie nodded and headed toward the house as Ricky, Kevin, Emily and Adam came around the corner of the barn.

"Daddy, can I ride with you?"

Kevin lifted his son to his shoulders. "Sure, but your uncle Adam is a better horseman than I am. Why don't you ride with him?" They disappeared inside the barn.

Alex took hold of Katarina's hand momentarily and slowed his pace as they headed for the corrals. "I'm glad you decided to come, Katarina. I wasn't so sure you would after what I said the other night. I thought sure you and Ron would have plans for the weekend."

"He didn't want to make the drive again so soon." Before she could stop, the bitter words slipped out.

Alex looked up the hill, his profile strong and rigid. "What is wrong with the man?" he muttered.

Katarina cocked her ear toward him. "Did you say something?"

Alex tugged her closer and whispered into her ear. "Yeah, that man is a total fool."

She lifted her chin and looked into his blue eyes, surprised to find his intense gaze fixed on hers. *Who's the fool here, God? What is stopping me from ending this farce of a relationship with Ron? Why can't I let myself follow my heart?*

Alex's lips brushed her forehead. He gently turned her, pulling her into the circle of his arms as he did so.

"C'mon, Uncle Alex and Auntie Kat! We'll race ya." Adam and Ricky's horse stepped out from around the barn just before Alex's lips could brush hers. Katarina jumped, surprised that Alex's hand was locked against her spine, holding her close.

Alex exhaled.

Adam guided the horse past Alex and Katarina. "Busted," Adam needled the couple, and laughed. "Think you can handle Gertrude *and* Star, Alex?"

"Not a problem." He let Katarina loose and led the way into the barn. Alex saddled the two mares and offered Katarina a hand up.

They trotted through the pasture, waiting impatiently for Gertrude to realize it wasn't time to graze. Adam stepped his horse up next to Katarina and showed her how to keep Gertrude's attention off the grass.

"I'm not going anywhere. Why don't you two give them a run?" Adam said to his brothers.

"You all right, Katarina?" The warmth of Alex's smile echoed in his voice.

She couldn't deny the confidence he'd just handed her. "I'm fine—you go ahead."

Katarina watched Alex and Star race Kevin and his mount, Cody, across the pasture then disappear into the trees. She felt the awareness spread through her body just watching Alex ride. He looked like a natural, not someone who hadn't ridden in ten years.

Suddenly Gertrude, feeling left out, took off at a gallop up the hill after them. *"Whoa!"*

Gertrude ignored her and ran right under a ponderosa.

Katarina lowered her voice, pulled the reins and lay back trying to duck under the prickly branch. *"Whoa!"* She came to a sudden stop.

Adam rode up beside her. "Are you all right?"

Katarina took a deep breath as she pulled herself upright. "I think so. I don't think sweet old Gertrude likes me much."

"That was *neat*, Katarina. Can you do it again?" Ricky's eyes were opened wide, as if he thought she'd done it on purpose.

Adam chuckled. "You did great, Katarina. I can't imagine what Gert thought she was doing. She hasn't run like that in a year." He guided them back to the barn and helped Katarina dismount.

Despite "sweet old" Gertrude's antics, Adam proclaimed Katarina a fine rider when the family gathered around the campfire that night.

The next evening was celebrated with an ornately decorated birthday cake and a horse-drawn hayride up the hill to watch the fireworks from the surrounding towns.

Everyone "oohed" and "aahed" except Alex. He was on edge, watching the land, not the sky. "What's wrong?" Katarina whispered.

"It's that time of year, I guess. Fireworks are trouble waiting to happen. The whole area is like a tinderbox waiting to ignite. Over that hill is a campground. Hear the fireworks?"

She looked around in silence as the rest of the family continued to enjoy the display. A while later, they were ready to head back when Katarina noticed an orange glow on the horizon. "Alex, look."

"We've got a fire west of Carter Lake. Get us home, Adam. I have my gear in my truck."

The wagon jolted forward, and they had a very bouncy ride back to the ranch. Emily looked as if she was going to be sick, while the others tried to determine exactly where the fire was located.

Adam pulled into the yard and Alex jumped off the wagon. "Call the fire department. I'm heading out."

Kevin and the twins' husbands followed. "Wait a minute, we'll come with you. Let me get a few more shovels."

"I'll be there in a bit," Adam added. After he put the team and wagon away, he jumped in his own four-wheel-drive truck and headed up the hill to help.

Millie ran inside to make the call, and sirens soon wailed in the distance. She started a campfire in the

pit as soon as she hung up the phone, and the
women and children roasted marshmallows. Two
hours later, the men returned black with soot from
head to toe. She watched Adam walk to the campfire, sit down and stretch out his long legs on the
grass next to her. Four different variations of the
same story were told, one from each firefighter. All
gave credit to Alex for his leadership and instruction
to the rookies.

Alex and his brothers took turns cleaning up before turning in for the night. She felt like a coward
slipping into her bed while he showered. She wasn't
ready to make the kind of decision he seemed to
want from her.

Katarina felt a chill and realized it had nothing to
do with the cool mountain air. As they'd watched
the orange glow on the horizon, she'd realized how
dangerous fire fighting could be. And this blaze was
nothing compared to the fires Alex usually battled.
Fires had been his life. His passion. Could he ever
really give that up?

Katarina pushed harder, putting in longer hours
getting ready for a doll show at the end of July; yet
even her fatigue was pushed aside by another electrical storm one night. She couldn't erase that image
of a lightning strike starting another fire, forcing
Alex to return to smoke jumping.

Alex had stayed at Adam's ranch for a couple of
extra days after the camp-out to oversee the digging
and pouring of the foundation. He and Adam had

given everyone a guided tour of the blueprints. Alex's excitement over the log structure was second only to his youngest brother's. Katarina had had a wonderful weekend, in spite of the fears the fire sparked inside.

Trying to put Alex out of her mind, Katarina dug through her latest shipment of Christmas fabrics and matched fabrics with designs for Sylvia to work on. She yawned.

"Aren't you feeling well, Katarina? You don't look like yourself."

Katarina tried to ignore the soreness when she swallowed. "Probably just tired."

The plump mother of three teenagers felt Katarina's head. "You have a fever. Why don't you go back to bed? I see what you're wanting on these dresses. I'll be fine. If I finish early, I'll start stuffing bodies for you."

"Thanks, Syl. Maybe a nap will help."

Chapter Sixteen

Alex stayed at the ranch until the end of the week, then returned to catch up on paperwork and gather supplies he'd need to take back after the weekend.

"How's Kat feeling?" Kevin asked.

Alex pushed the button on the copier. "Feeling? What's wrong with her?"

His younger brother chuckled. "You're living with her. I'd assume you knew."

"Correction, we share a house—temporarily. That doesn't mean we keep tabs on each other. I've been at Adam's all week getting things under way. I just came back to pick up a few things." He gathered the bids and stacked them. "The house didn't look like she was even home when I dropped by this morning. So what am I supposed to know?"

Kevin moved to the desk. "I don't know. She called Emily last night. I didn't hang around to see if it was a personal or professional call, to be honest.''

Maybe that was why it didn't look as if she'd been out of her room. And all this time he'd assumed she was avoiding him. ''Maybe I'd better go check on her.''

''I thought there's nothing going on between you two?'' Kevin gibed.

''I'm concerned. Is there something wrong with that?''

Kevin raised his hands in front of him. ''Don't get testy. Take the day off if you'll feel better. And tell Kat hi for me, too.''

Alex backtracked out of the tiny trailer his brother now called an office. Why couldn't Kevin just accept that he and Katarina were friends? From the looks of things, that's all they would ever be. It had been a week and his ego was still bruised from her asking him to leave the gazebo.

He turned into the cul-de-sac and pulled into the driveway. He simply thought Katarina was drawing her boundaries. He'd decided it was for the best. He didn't want to make more of their relationship than there was. She was still committed to Ron.

So where was Ron when Katarina needed help? Why wasn't Ron the one running up the stairs looking like a lovesick fool? Alex stopped. Why was he doing this? She was spoken for. There was no hope of anything between them.

He walked into the foyer and went to her bedroom

door. It remained closed, just as it had been when he left a week ago and when he'd arrived this morning. He lifted his fist to knock, then stopped. Maybe she was drawing the line, just as he'd asked her to.

He checked the garage. Nothing was out of place. He ran to the basement and into her painting "studio." Brushes were dry. No trace of turpentine odor. She hadn't painted in a while.

Alex returned to the main floor. Was Kevin goading him on? Had Katarina really called to consult with Dr. Emily? Maybe she'd simply been asking for sisterly advice. He tapped his knuckles on her door. If he made a fool of himself, at least it was for a benevolent reason. She didn't answer. He hesitantly reached for the knob, then stopped.

Katarina had every right not to answer.

Alex went across the hall and looked in her sewing room. The seamstress had obviously been here. He read her note to Katarina. "I finished the list of dresses we discussed and sewed two bodies. I couldn't find..." Alex skimmed the rest of the note.... "Hope you get feeling better. See you Monday."

Katarina was sick and too proud to ask for help. He took his cell phone from his belt and dialed her number. After the fifth ring, she answered, then went into a coughing fit. At least, he assumed it was her. Kevin's concern was far understated.

"Katarina? It's Alex. I'm in the living room, and I'm here to check on you. Kevin said you're sick."

There was a crash on the other end. He pressed End and ran to her room, relieved when the knob turned.

Katarina was huddled under two layers of comforters, her cheeks flushed and her body curled into a fetal position. Her eyes opened slightly, then drooped closed.

"Katarina..." he gasped. He touched her forehead and pulled his hand back. "You're burning up!" He reached for the covers and pulled off the top layer.

"No. I'm cold," she croaked, then began coughing.

He looked around. There wasn't a glass, or any sign of medication. "Do you have a thermometer?" No response.

Alex went to the kitchen and brought her a drink. "Come on, Katarina, sit up and take a drink. We need to get some fluids in you."

Katarina turned her head.

He found Katarina's phone on the floor between the bed and the end table. That must have been the crash he'd heard. When he reached Emily she asked him to bring Katarina in to the office.

"Could you come here? I can't even get her to sit up to take a drink. It doesn't look like she's had a thing to drink since she came home four days ago. She's set up a vaporizer, the room's a sauna and she's burning up."

Emily gave him instructions and agreed to be there in less than an hour. Alex searched for a thermometer, trying to ignore her persistent cough. He couldn't find anything to give her for the fever, then realized he wouldn't be able get it down her anyway.

The doorbell rang, and he was relieved to see Emily, even though she started drilling him for information he couldn't supply.

"I just got home today," Alex explained. "Adam and I worked on the plans until late last night. I had no idea Katarina was sick till Kevin mentioned it this morning when I went in. She seemed fine last weekend."

As they both went to Katarina's room, Alex tried to explain their disagreement, and that he thought she was still avoiding him.

One look at her sister and Emily started pulling things from her bag. "She was pushing too hard. I've tried to tell her she can't do that."

"I tried to tell her the same thing." *Among other things.* "That was some of what we argued about. She told me it was none of my business."

Right now he just wanted to know what was wrong with Katarina.

His sister-in-law sat on the edge of the bed. "Kat, it's Emily. I'm going to take your temperature and do a strep test. We'll know something soon, honey." She placed some gadget in Katarina's ear and removed it when it beeped.

Alex stared at the contraption, suddenly feeling like a total idiot. "What's that?"

"A thermometer." She glanced at it, and started

yanking the remaining covers from Katarina. "Good grief, Katarina, you're cooking yourself. Take these," she said, handing him another quilt and a blanket. Dr. Emily checked Katarina's pulse.

Alex tossed the comforter to the floor. "What happened to the little glass thing you put in the mouth?"

Emily laughed. "Ancient history. We have to get her temperature down. Do you know where there's a basin or bowl I can use to sponge her off?"

"No, but I'll find something." Alex returned with a bowl of tepid water and grabbed one of the pretty washcloths from the basket in Katarina's bathroom. Emily took the culture, then placed the swab in a tube and pinched the end. Katarina started coughing again. "Let's get some fresh air in here. Heavens sakes alive, Katarina, it's perfect breeding grounds for germs."

Emily turned to him. "If you'll make her some juice, I'll change her clothes. Then let's move her onto the sofa while her room airs out. I don't want her in a draft. We should also change the sheets."

Alex closed the door behind him, went to the kitchen and took the juice from the refrigerator. He quickly jotted down a list of groceries to pick up when he had a chance.

He ran upstairs and got a pillow from his bed and clean linens from the closet. Just as his mother had when he was a boy, he spread the sheet on the sofa and placed a clean pillowcase on the pillow. He thought a minute, then ran back up the stairs to see if she kept extra sheets for her bed in her room or in that same upstairs linen closet. This house, while very nice, was about as functional as a bunkhouse.

"Alex. We're ready. She won't wake. If you wouldn't mind helping her to the other room, I umm...shouldn't." Emily's hand brushed her abdomen. "I shouldn't lift her."

He looked at his sister-in-law, stunned. Had he been here, away from his own life, that long? Making a quick calculation, he estimated Kevin and Emily had been married just under two months now. "You mean...you're pregnant?"

Emily's face matched her red hair. "A honeymoon baby. I just took the test yesterday. We're not making it public knowledge yet, but I don't want you to think I'm being a wimp. Normally I'd try lifting her myself."

"Of course you can't take a chance. Congratulations."

"Thank you." Emily smiled. "Let Kevin tell you about the baby, please. He's dying to break the news, and I've begged him to wait until the first trimester is over."

Silently he nodded. The last thing he was thinking about right now was ruining his brother's secret.

"I have the sofa ready for her." Alex cradled her in his arms, one hand under Katarina's shoulders and one beneath her knees. "Come on, sweetie."

He carefully eased his way through the door.

Looking at the seemingly lifeless form in his arms, he couldn't believe it was spunky, vivacious Katarina. How could a few days change a person so drastically? He instinctively pulled her closer, wishing he could be the man she wanted to protect and take care of her.

And in the meantime, where was the man who was supposed to be doing just that? Did Katarina even realize Ron should be helping her through tough times like this? He realized that because their father had walked out, all three sisters had a serious independent streak in them. Self-preservation, he guessed. "Is she even conscious?"

There was a long pause before Emily answered. "For all practical purposes, no."

"What's wrong with her?"

"I don't think it's strep. Without her cooperation, I couldn't get a clear diagnosis from listening to her lungs, but I think I heard a crackle in her left lung. The cough alone is a pretty good indicator of pneumonia. X rays will give us a definite answer."

"I'll be glad to take her. What time?"

"Thank you so much, Alex. I'll call the clinic to see when we can get her in. My only other choice would have been to call an ambulance."

"If she has pneumonia, shouldn't she stay in the hospital?"

"Unless there are other complications, I think we can handle it here, if you don't mind. After we get her medicated, she'll sleep most of the time. I guarantee she'll get more rest here than at the hospital. I'll come by a few times a day to check on her, and if you could do the same, she should be okay. I could hire someone to come in and help her for a few days.''

''You don't need to hire anyone, I'll be here.''

Emily smiled as she moved to the kitchen. ''I see you have a list started already. I'll run to the store to get these things and get her prescriptions filled. Call if you think of anything else.''

He nodded, then took the sheets to the basement and started the laundry. He stepped outside for a breath of fresh air. *God, I shouldn't be feeling so protective of Katarina.* He reviewed the list of reasons he shouldn't let himself fall in love with her. She was too young, and he couldn't pretend the nine-year difference in their age didn't exist. She bubbled over with optimism, and he could barely manage pessimistic realism. She longed to experience life, and he was ready to settle down. He watched the summer breeze rustling the trees. ''What am I going to do? It just isn't fair, God. Why now? Why her?''

''Ahem.''

He jumped at the sound of Emily's voice. ''Oh. I thought you were gone.''

Emily smiled. ''Kat finally woke up and needed to use the rest room, so I waited to make sure she made it back to the sofa okay.'' Emily closed the sliding door behind her. ''Why don't we talk?''

He suddenly felt like a sixteen-year-old all over again having *that* talk with his mother. "I'm sorry Emily. I'll get out of her life as soon as possible."

"Why? Is that what you want?"

"I don't want to hurt her. She...has Ron."

The redhead laughed. "I'm the wrong person to talk to about Ron, but *please* don't leave on his account. Do you love Katarina?"

Was there nothing shy about these sisters? "I haven't even answered that question for myself, Em." He felt his heartbeat racing. "I'm the last person she needs. But I don't understand why that boyfriend of hers isn't in the picture right now."

"That I won't comment on. As for you, Alex, I will say to be sure what you want. My sister is an incurable romantic. While she, too, denies there's anything between you two, I don't believe a word of it. I suspect that if you were two years older instead of nine, there'd be no hesitation, for either of you. Don't get me wrong, I think you and Katarina would be great together." Before he could stop her, she rushed on. "It isn't because you're too old, or anything else. Katarina is terrified of looking for a father figure. She was engaged to an older man once. Most of the men in her life have been very willing to be the father she never had."

He thought a moment. "That's the last thing I'm feeling. She's at a totally different place in her life."

"Did you ever consider that she looks at your life as an endless adventure? To a woman who never experienced anything more adventurous than an amusement park, jumping out of airplanes and climbing mountains is very appealing."

"Ron should be the one to show her what life has to offer."

Emily laughed. "Ron won't be that man. You're not listening to me, Alex. She doesn't want to marry Ron. And no matter how much she says so, it won't happen. He's a security blanket. And he's four hundred miles away."

"Then again, I don't want a relationship based only upon a need for adventure."

"Life with the right person is one adventure after another, whether it's cooking breakfast together or climbing Longs Peak. With the right person, the years between you melt away, and the only thing that matters is your love for one another."

He hated to admit Emily was right. When he and Katarina were together, he felt younger. And she made his world seem new again. While he was grounded in reality, she taught him to dream. "I'll think about it, Emily. There's still the matter of Ron. In the meantime, it's Katarina I'm concerned about."

"I called the clinic and was able to schedule her for an appointment at one. Can you bring her in?"

"Of course. What do I do until then?"

"I couldn't get her to swallow pills for her fever, so I gave her a liquid medication." She looked at her watch. "I'll have the groceries and her prescriptions ready when you come."

"Good. I'll call Kevin, tell him I'll be out for the day." Alex stepped into the kitchen and poured a glass of juice for Katarina.

"Thank you, Alex. She hates hospitals. I appreciate your help in taking care of her."

"Thank you for everything, Emily."

"I hope our talk helped."

"I hope so, too." He smiled, still holding Katarina's drink. He followed Emily outside to find an extra straw from a fast-food restaurant in the glove box of his truck. Once he found one, he took the juice to her. Her color looked better already. Whether it was the fresh air, her fever was down already, or simply that he felt comforted knowing she was being cared for now, he wasn't sure. He knelt next to the sofa and coaxed her lips around the straw.

"Katarina, take a drink. It's your favorite, cherry juice." She took a sip, then another. He waited patiently as she finished all of it. Between drinks, she coughed weakly, in obvious pain with each one. "Good job, Kat. I'll be in the other room if you need me." She was already asleep, and he eased the straw from her mouth.

He felt her forehead and brushed the damp hair from her brow. His heart had never hurt like this. It had to be love. And as long as Ron was in the picture, how could he do anything about it?

Just remembering Emily's comments made him angry. What did she mean, Ron wouldn't be the man to share her love for the adventures in life? What sort of man was he, and why did Katarina insist she was going to marry him?

He went downstairs and moved the sheets from the washer to the dryer. As he straightened her room, he noticed Ron's picture on her dresser. What was it Emily had said about him? He was her security blanket. Was he wealthy? Powerful? What did Katarina see in him that her sister didn't?

Figuring Katarina kept a list of phone numbers by her phone, Alex looked until he found Ron's number. Even if he didn't want the man there, Katarina loved him, and he should be here to comfort her now. How was it Katarina had said it at the wedding? *I'm as good as engaged already.* Alex shoved the memory away. "Good for you, Kat. Let's just see how engaged Ron is." He dialed and waited. By the time the secretary transferred him to the man, Alex was fighting the urge to hang up. Why was he giving Ron another chance?

When Alex hung up the phone, he was madder than ever. Katarina's notable "fiancé" couldn't be bothered with her when she was ill. He'd "rather wait until she's well enough to enjoy my visit."

"No way am I going to give her your best," Alex grumbled. "If you can't do that for yourself, there's no way I'm doing it for you."

Chapter Seventeen

Alex lowered his voice. "You can't keep covering your pain with humor, Katarina. I want you to talk about this."

She ignored him and continued to cook the ground beef for tacos. This was her first day out of bed. Alex had been a mother hen for over a week. Why couldn't he just leave her alone and let her live her own life?

"Where was Ron, Katarina? If the man loves you enough to spend the rest of his life with you, why wasn't he here when you needed him? Other than your usual Friday-at-four flowers, he hasn't even been in touch."

"Stop it. He didn't even know I was sick." Considering the anger in Alex's words, the tenderness in his expression confused her. She stirred the hamburger, then grated the cheddar cheese.

Alex leaned one hip against the edge of the counter. He closed his eyes and lifted his chin.

Is he totally frustrated with me or saying a quick prayer? Kat pushed past Alex to drain the ground beef.

"He knew from the very first day. I called him."

"Who asked you to do that?"

"I thought he might want to drop everything and come take care of you himself." Alex didn't wait to press the issue. "Where will the Boy Scout be when you have kids who need their father, Kat? You of all people can't pretend that doesn't matter."

She glared at him. "That's a low blow."

"And accusing me of wanting to be your father wasn't?" He paced the room like a caged animal. "Maybe it's about time someone opened your eyes to the truth. The man isn't going to change once you marry him. Maybe you don't even want children. Maybe you don't care if your husband loves you, but you should. Marriage is not only depending on each other, but giving and sharing. And I don't see Ron doing much of either."

"What in the world do you know about how Ron feels about me?" Katarina turned to face Alex. "Maybe he's—"

"His actions speak for themselves. Anyone who doesn't even call to see how you're feeling doesn't deserve you. And anyone content with seeing their love no more often than once a month hasn't found the love of his life."

"Oh?" Suddenly her mouth went dry. Was that why Alex never stayed in Loveland longer than a few nights? She felt her heart race with hope that someone would actually consider *her* important enough to arrange his schedule around and not just fit her in when it was convenient. *God, is it Alex I've saved myself for? It's so sudden. I've known Ron for years...*

Alex took a step closer. He reached around her, turned off the stove and offered her a sympathetic smile. "I don't want to see you hurt. You say he's going to be popping the question soon. I want you to go into this with your eyes open."

Katarina was torn between wanting to repay the pain Alex was inflicting on her, and wanting him even more because he cared enough to be honest. She closed her eyes, her head swirling with doubts.

What woman wouldn't be light-headed over the kind of attention Alex was paying to her? Who wouldn't be flattered and attracted to him? But could she take a risk like giving up a long-term relationship for a man she'd known only a few weeks?

"Who are we trying to fool, Katarina?"

She stared at him. "I don't believe I've tried to fool anyone. I've been honest with you." There were so many things to consider before taking a chance with Alex. If they became serious, would it be difficult on the families to have sisters and brothers to contend with? Would the age difference become a problem? Could she learn to be more open with her feelings? He wasn't the type of man to settle for a superficial relationship. Already he had broken through every protective barrier she'd ever mastered.

Alex's gaze dropped to her locket and he touched it gingerly, his eyes studying it with a curious intensity. He stared at her in waiting silence.

Katarina felt like a breathless girl of eighteen again. His nearness made her senses spin, yet she trusted him as she never had another man. She inhaled a slow and shallow breath, careful not to start another coughing spasm. "Emily gave that to me when she went away to medical school. Go ahead and open it."

"That's okay."

With that simple gesture of trust, he unlocked her heart and soul. She reached up and opened it. "Lisa and Emily. They are my soul mates."

She could almost see the relief in his blue eyes. The worry lines by his mouth softened.

"I hope there's room for another soul mate in there, Katarina." He touched a whisper of a kiss on her forehead and stepped back. "Until there's a ring on your finger, I refuse to give up hope that we can become more than friends. And I promise, I won't make it easy for you to walk away."

She had long ago tried to convince herself that near kisses and embraces would never make her swoon, yet from Alex, she had no defenses. The man broke all her other rules—why not this one, too?

Katarina hadn't realized she was holding her breath until she exhaled too quickly and ended up coughing, an annoying residual effect from her pneumonia. She put an ice chip in her mouth and let the slow release of cold liquid soothe her throat.

"Go rest. I'll finish supper."

The call came early afternoon. The offer she'd been praying diligently about, waiting for, working toward for four years. Unique Designs wanted to buy her company—dolls, designs, stock, and hire her as a full-time consultant. The deal included a benefit package and meant no more traveling, no more trying to sell her wares, no more bookkeeping. All of the fun and no more headaches, as Ron would say.

There was only one hitch in the deal. She'd have to move to Arkansas.

She dialed number after number, unable to reach anyone. She was itching to share her news. Emily was working late. Lisa hadn't returned her call. Her mother was in meetings. Kevin and Alex were at Adam's putting in another long day. The afternoon dragged on in silence.

That left Ron. Her heart sank at the thought of telling him. His strategy had worked even better than they'd expected, as she hadn't dreamed anyone would offer her such a lucrative salary to design exclusively for them.

Katarina went to the sewing room. Just the sight

of the doll clothes brought tears to her eyes. This was her dream come true. After only four years, Kat's Kreations would be sold nationally and internationally.

Her tears caught her off guard. She looked around and felt everything close in. She ran to her room and closed the door. *How can I cry over something I've wanted so badly, God? You've answered my prayers so generously, and I'm crying? What's wrong with me?*

There was a soft knock on the door, followed by Alex's deep voice. "Katarina?"

She sniffed and buried her face in her hands, wiping the tears from her eyes. She didn't want anyone to see her like this.

"May I come in?"

She started sobbing again.

Alex was sure he'd heard crying. He opened the door and peeked inside. From the way Katarina jumped he must have surprised her. She immediately turned away, but not before he saw her puffy eyes. He couldn't hold himself back. He walked around to the far side of the bed, sat next to her and pulled her close. To his surprise, she wrapped her arms tightly around him and rested her head on his chest. "Katarina, what's wrong?" He rubbed her back to calm her down.

She sobbed once more, then regained control. "I have an offer for Kat's Kreations."

His hand stopped. He looked her in the eye. "You don't seem too happy."

Katarina untangled herself from him and pasted a smile on her face. "Of course I'm happy."

Alex laughed. "I may have only known you a few weeks, but I can tell there's something very wrong here. What is it?"

"I think it's just an overload of emotions."

He leaned back and examined her closely. "Yes, I see it now. You're just bubbling over with them."

"Alex..." she chided him, stretching his name almost into two words.

"Katarina..." he mimicked. "Be honest. What is it you don't like about the deal?"

Katarina shrugged. She listed all the benefits of what sounded like a very profitable deal. "I guess I'm feeling a little possessive," she said, then hesitated. "I don't want this to sound arrogant, but, well, it's my company. They don't just want a few dolls, they want it all. Even my name." Tears spilled onto her cheeks.

He grinned, trying to lighten her mood. "It is a beautiful name. I'd kind of like to have Katarina for my own, too. You should feel flattered to be in such great demand."

She nudged his shoulder with hers. "Did you feel that way about your dad's company when you sold it?"

"Sure I did. It's the main reason I went into smoke jumping. I had to do something totally..."

"Reckless?"

"I was going to say different. I thought it was sort of daring before I got into it. Then I realized it's an overglamorized job from the public view. It was a great break from what I really wanted to do, which was build."

"And now you want to go back?"

He nodded.

Katarina wiped her eyes, yet tears streamed calmly down her face. "I hoped maybe one day my father would recognize my name out there and come find us girls." She started sobbing again. "I want him to be proud of me."

Alex wiped the tears from Katarina's cheeks while fighting back tears of his own. "I'm sure he is, Kat. Until he can tell you for himself, your heavenly Father is there for you. I don't know what I'd have done without God after my dad died. I'd pushed Kevin away, Mom had her own grief to deal with, Grandpa was distraught that his son had died before him, and my other grandparents had already passed on."

"I just wish sometimes that I didn't care, that the longing to please him would go away."

"When you were a little girl, did you blame yourself for him leaving?"

She nodded. "I made him all sorts of things, hoping that if he just knew how much I loved him, he'd come home. After a few months I lost hope of seeing him again, and started making animals and dolls out of old scraps for Lisa to play with. I liked how happy they made her.'' Katarina pulled one of her dolls into her lap. Was her choice of profession also due to her father? Did she create dolls in order to attempt to mend some broken path in her lonely childhood? ''What about Emily and Lisa? How do they feel about your dad?''

''Emily picked up the role of caregiver, since Mom had never worked and suddenly had to find a job. The first few years, Mom worked three of them. I think Emily was so mad at Dad that it was a relief to shut out her feelings for him. Emily was determined to make sure she didn't ever have to rely on a husband for an income.'' She looked up apologetically.

''We can't handle that for Kevin and Emily. They're dealing with that themselves. But don't ever feel bad about trying to defend your sister.'' Alex looked over at the other dolls on Katarina's pillow.

''Lisa was only two when he left. She went to a neighbor's when Emily and I were in school, and Mom would bring her home in time for dinner, then tuck us in before she left for her night jobs. I doubt Lisa really spends much time thinking about it, to be honest. In a sense, she really never knew what it was like to have a father, so it didn't bother her. So I guess that means I'm the only warped sister.''

Alex pulled her close, wishing he could ease her pain. ''You're not warped. You're a very determined young woman who turned something comforting into an enterprising business. Your dolls make people happy. God gave you a wonderful gift, Katarina. There's no reason you shouldn't take pride in using it in the way He intended it.'' He looked into his lap and found the doll he'd been looking at on the pillow a minute ago. He didn't remember picking it up. He looked at Katarina. ''Do you name all of them?''

''Each design has a name. This is Melissa, and the one you're holding is Bye-Bye.''

Beautiful lavender-blue eyes, blonde hair and a pretty pout. He noticed a tear in the corner of the doll's eye. Katarina set her doll on the bed and moved to lean against the dresser.

''Then you think I should accept the job offer?''

''I think you're consulting the wrong man. I follow a strict code—don't give opinions on matters that should be discussed between a woman and her fiancé.''

If possible, the tears had changed her eyes to an almost purplish color. ''What if she wasn't involved—with someone else. What would you tell her then?''

Was he imagining it, or had he seen a hint of a smile on her lips? She was so incredibly beautiful. ''I'd tell her to follow her heart.''

''I don't know what it's telling me. Please, Alex, give me your opinion. Just an opinion. It *doesn't* mean I'm going to do it.''

Alex's lips curved into a gentle smile as he shook

his head. "Kat, do you want me to tell you what you should do? Or do you want me to tell you what *I* want you to do?"

"Is there a difference?"

"You're darn right there is. I have no right to tell you what's right for you. For that matter, no one should tell you what to do. And, unfortunately, I'm not in a position to say what I'd like you to do."

"You're doing this on purpose. To drive me crazy."

"That makes two of us, then."

Katarina had never been so confused. It had been weeks since she'd seen Ron. Was it just loneliness that drew her to Alex? After all, he was suddenly her closest confidant. They'd spent every evening talking. He'd shown her how to put her work away and listen to her heart. How to rely on God, the Father.

"Does this mean you haven't told Ron?"

She shook her head.

"Hmm." Alex's dark eyebrows rose. He stood and gently placed the baby doll back on the pillow. "Then you'd best be having a lengthy talk with God. Figure out just what it is you do want." He proceeded to the kitchen. She followed him, the electricity so intense between them that the very air around them seemed to spark.

Was Alex telling her he wanted to be the man she consulted with? Or was he, as usual, just being "Mr. Nice Guy"? He was nothing like Ron. And the more she thought about Ron, the more depressed she became. If she sold her company, he would expect her to return to him right away. Was that the only reason she was afraid to make the call?

Or was it something else altogether? Did she really want to sell her company? What if she didn't want to move? *God, I don't know what to do. Please help me come to the right decision.*

"Since you're not going to help me make this decision, I guess I'll go for a walk."

"Sounds like a good idea. In case you were thinking of going by Emily's, they won't be home tonight."

She turned to him and put her hands on her hips. "I'm not going to Emily's, for your information."

Alex shrugged innocently. "Just thought maybe…"

He infuriated her. "Don't worry yourself about this anymore. I'll make my *own* decision. I won't bother you again." She spun around and headed for the door.

"Katarina." Alex closed the distance between them and turned her to face him. With a hand on each of her shoulders, he looked her in the eye. "I know what you're going through. It's something you can't let anyone else decide for you. You brought Kat's Kreations this far, and you're perfectly capable of taking it to whatever heights you want it to go."

Chapter Eighteen

Katarina rolled over in her bed and hugged the extra pillow to her body. It was only six, still a bit early to get up. For two days now she'd looked forward to spending the entire day with Alex. He'd insisted some fresh air and sunshine would be good for her. A quick glance outside put an immediate end to the sunshine part. The morning sky had an eerie gloom to it. Just her luck, after a record-setting dry summer, that Mother Nature had picked today to send the much-needed rain. She snuggled down and closed her eyes again.

She had spent the majority of the past two weeks in bed tormented by her growing feelings for Alex. He had taken two days off work while she was at her worst, and had been home promptly at six every night since then. Between Emily and Sylvia, the two made sure Katarina got plenty of rest. Even without their strict ministration, she had no strength to push herself.

Alex had prepared several meals and placed them in the freezer for her. He'd cleaned the house and made sure she had clean laundry. Each day he brought her a fresh glass of juice before leaving for work, and insisted she get outside to enjoy a few minutes of fresh air with him in the evening. Never before had she felt so cherished...in every sense of the word.

The weekend before, her insurance settlement had arrived. Knowing how anxious she was to have her own transportation again, Alex had taken notes on what she was looking for, then went scouting for a new vehicle. After looking at all the options, she'd purchased a minivan with plenty of cargo room. He'd suggested they take it out for a trial run today.

After much thought, Katarina had decided to counter the offer made by the toy company. If it hadn't been for Alex refusing to give her advice, she'd probably have taken the offer at face value, take it or leave it. The confidence he'd instilled in her in the past few weeks was a gift she could never forget. She didn't expect to hear from Unique Designs now until Monday.

She looked at the clock again, and decided seven was as long as she could stay in bed. For the first day in two weeks she felt energetic. After her shower, she pulled on a pair of jeans and a sweater, then went into the kitchen. There was no coffee in the pot.

The house was still. Surely Alex was awake. She looked up to the loft. His door was open, as it had been day and night since her illness. "Alex?" she called weakly. A burning sensation settled at the bottom of her stomach as she remembered the first morning after her father had walked out on her family.

She walked to the foot of the stairs. "Alex, are you here?" *He has no obligations to me. Still, he was the one who invited me to go to the mountains with him today.* She recalled their conversation about her father. Had that scared him away? *Don't be ridiculous, Katarina.*

"This just isn't like him," she whispered. She forced herself up the stairs to tease him for over-sleeping. She hesitated just shy of the opening. "Alex?"

She peeked into the master bedroom. The covers had been tossed over the pillows. The room was otherwise neat and tidy, and pretty much empty.

She went back down the stairs, through the mud-room and into the garage. His truck was gone. His boots weren't on the garage step where he left them each night after work. All of his work clothes…gone.

He was gone.

"He can't…walk…out," she said, gulping back

tears. "There's nothing to walk out on. We aren't dating. We're nothing more than friends."

She heard the phone ring. Her feet were planted in fear. Finally Katarina moved toward the phone, but not before the answering machine clicked on.

"Katarina, it's Alex. I didn't want you to find a note. I'm sorry about today. There's a fire just west of Adam's ranch on forest service land. Adam needed help. The other crews are jumping into big fires."

She heaved a sigh of relief and picked up the phone, though the machine continued to record. "When did they call? I didn't hear the phone."

"A little before three. I'm relieved I caught it before it woke you. I can't talk long, but I wanted to tell you myself." Katarina could hear the remorse in his voice. The static from his phone was cutting out. "I didn't know whether to wake you or leave a note.... It's strange, Kat. I don't know what the situation calls for. We're just friends."

"I know."

He lowered his voice. "It feels like more than friendship. I want it to be more."

"I know, Alex."

"I know it's only been a few weeks. We don't even know how long either of us will be in Springville."

Tears stung her eyes. She hadn't told Alex that one stipulation of the offer was that she relocate.

"Does this mean you're going back to Montana soon?"

The silence was so long she thought they'd lost the connection. "I've tried not to notice how bad the fires are, but they need an experienced crew leader out here. Kevin insisted I go."

I need you, too.

"I'll be back in town as soon as we get this fire out. That should be by the end of the day. Then I'll need to pick up my clean clothes before I head out."

She looked out the window and realized the haze wasn't from clouds or the hope of rain, but smoke from the fire Alex was fighting. He was forty miles away. She could only imagine what Alex was dealing with now. "I'll see you when you get here, then."

"And Katarina, stay inside today. This smoke will irritate your lungs." He paused. "G'bye."

She let out a deep sigh. "I will, Alex. Bye." The machine clicked off when she hung up.

All day long his voice stayed with her alternately warming her heart and sending a chill of warning to keep up her protective shield—just in case.

Exactly what did Alex want? What did she want? All her life she'd dreamed of a knight in shining armor whisking her away from her problems and insecurities. Was Alex that man?

Disappointment consumed her. She thought back to Alex's comment about Ron being content with the distance between them. Suddenly she understood. It didn't bother her that Ron wasn't around, yet she'd come to look forward to the end of the day when Alex came home from work.

Though she tried to recall how she'd felt when she and Ron were in the same town, she couldn't pull up any memories of feeling like this. Was Alex right? Did he look forward to coming home each night? Did he miss her the way she did him?

She wanted Alex here with her today. *Every* day, she realized. What if he decided not to come back after the fire season ended? That could be almost two more months. Was it too late to change her counteroffer?

Alex felt terrible that he'd had to run out on Katarina. She sounded as if she understood, but then again, this was a woman who had spent her life covering her pain with humor. And convincingly so.

They had to get this fire out right away. He had to see her. Had to convince her that he would come back. That he would always come back. *Don't let Katarina run from me, Father. Let me have a chance to tell her just how much I love her.* He bellowed orders to the volunteers who were doing their best to scratch a fire line around the blaze. It was inaccessible to the local fire department. And not serious enough yet to warrant forest service action.

Adam gave him a look of reprimand for the harsh tone. "What has you so irritated?"

"This wasn't exactly how I planned to spend the day."

His younger brother gave Alex a look of probing query. "I promised to bring Katarina to the mountains today."

"You're getting mighty attached to her, aren't you? Seems a little self-destructive, since she's seeing someone else. Isn't it?"

Alex swung his Pulaski and tugged the grass and roots loose. The last thing he needed was a reminder of the futility of the situation. Especially after today. Walking out on her was probably the worst thing he could have done. He should have stayed, explained to her in person. Told her before he left all that he planned to tell her this afternoon—that he wanted to marry her. That he wanted to spend each and every day extinguishing the embers of fear that smoldered in her mind. That he wanted to be the man she could depend on, consulted with, to show her the world, if that was what she wanted.

He'd wanted to tell her he would never leave her. *I'm going to lose her. She trusted me to be there, and I wasn't. Just like her dad. Why did this fire have to start today, Father?*

To teach you to trust in Me, my son. Hand Me your fears, Alex. You've trusted Me to care for you in all of your days. Am I not gracious enough to care for the love of your life, as well?

Alex focused on the fire, ashamed of himself for feeling so selfish.

He heard Adam's laughter. "Whoa, brother. I think you're too late."

"Too late for what?"

"To put out the fire."

He looked around. They were making progress. Another hour or two, and they'd be on their way home. "What are you talking about?"

"The fire Katarina started."

Alex laughed. "And you know what? I hope it never goes out." He went back to work. "Now let's take care of this little problem here, so I can get home and tell her so."

Chapter Nineteen

Katarina opened the door, ready to greet Alex. Before her stood Ron, all six foot of sophistication and arrogance. Her jaw moved, but no sound escaped her mouth.

"Hi, darlin'," he said, sweeping her into his arms and pressing his lips to hers. "What's wrong, still not feeling well? I figured you ought to be ready for company by now."

She eased away. "Ron. I wasn't expecting you."

"Who were you expecting? That roommate of yours? It's a good thing I decided to surprise you, then, isn't it?" His gaze darted around the room, as if looking for Alex.

She'd never heard Ron talk like this. She stepped back. The question caught her off guard, as did Ron's visit. Alex's mother had called to say the fire was out and Alex was on his way. Katarina glanced at her watch.

"What's gotten into you?" She saw the skepticism in his eyes. "I would have thought you of all people would have a little more trust in me." *It's time for me to make a decision, Father. Please let me make the right one.*

Ron's eyes flashed in a familiar display of impatience. He took her gently into his embrace, and Katarina's courage waned. "I didn't say anything about not trusting you. After all, Katarina, we're both human. Of all people, I can certainly understand that."

"And what does that mean?" Her misgivings were multiplying by the minute.

"It means I'm willing to forgive whatever's been going on here. I understand the loneliness." His voice echoed like a bad dream. He reached into his pocket and Katarina turned away.

"You know I wouldn't succumb to temptation, Ron. Not with you, or anyone else. I've saved myself for my husband. No one is going to change that now."

"Does this look like a lack of trust?" Ron opened the tiny jewelry box, exposing an ostentatious diamond ring. "I've realized what a mistake it is for you to be here alone, especially now that you've sold your company."

"I've made a counteroffer."

"Well, maybe I can sweeten that decision," Ron

said, his words thin and hollow. "We may as well get married. I had the lawyer draw up a prenuptial agreement according to the offer, so there's nothing more to hold us back."

Katarina gulped. He wasn't even listening to her.

"I don't think this move has been good for you."

Shallow words from a shallow man. This has nothing to do with my company. How could I have been so blind, God?

"The counteroffer changes quite a few things, Ron. Even if I sell them some of my designs, I'll still continue the production of Kat's Kreations. I won't give them full rights to my own name. This is my company. It means more to me than money."

He stared at her in disbelief from under his craggy eyebrows. "I thought that was the point of selling, so you could stop all that drudgery and devote your time to us."

"That's obviously what you want," she challenged. "Did you ever think about what I want? I'm good at this, Ron—even if making dolls isn't the status you want."

As if he finally realized she wasn't backing down, his mission swayed. "I suppose you could still sell your little dolls if you simply can't part with the business. It isn't a bad sideline."

Katarina took a staggering breath and counted to ten. *Little dolls? A sideline?*

Behind her the front door opened and Alex stepped inside, carrying his red pack and yellow shirt. He pulled the sunglasses from his sunburned face and stopped suddenly, as if he were in the wrong house.

His green pants and T-shirt were smudged with soot, and the shadow of a beard completed the impressive image. Her eyes froze on his long, lean form. She felt a smile snuffing out the anger she was feeling toward Ron.

"Hi, Alex."

"Afternoon," he said hesitantly, his gaze darting from Ron to Katarina and back. He dropped his boots on the tiled floor in the foyer and edged his way to the stairs. "I see you have company. I'm sorry to interrupt. I'm just here for a short stopover."

"Oh? So soon? I thought you'd at least have time to grab a bite to eat."

"The Bear Creek fire has doubled again. They've called in all available firefighters. They don't want to take a chance of another disaster."

"I see." *This is who Alex MacIntyre really is. Daring, macho, in control. And what if he chooses to go back to fire fighting full-time? Is that a decision we could work through? Would I ever be able to overcome my fear of abandonment?*

She felt a hand slide around her waist and possessively pull her closer. "I'm Ron, Kat's fiancé."

The blood rushed from her face, and she felt the air whoosh from her lungs. She started coughing again.

Alex stepped back. "Must be all this dust. Sorry. I'll get out of here. It's the last thing your lungs need right now." Without any congratulations or further introductions, Alex turned and ran up the stairs, closing his bedroom door behind him.

Still coughing, Kat escaped into the kitchen for a glass of water. Tears burned her eyes.

"Katarina. Why don't you go change for dinner? I've made reservations."

"What's wrong with what I'm wearing?" She looked down at the brand-new rayon sundress.

"My parents are meeting us to celebrate," he retorted, as if that would impress her. "I'm going to get my bag and be right back."

Before she could argue, Ron went outside to his SUV.

Alex came downstairs and passed her in silence. Katarina followed him to the basement, thankful for a minute of privacy.

"Alex. I had no idea he was coming. And I haven't had time to talk to him yet."

"How long does it take to say no? Or maybe it's me you planned to dump." He reached into the dryer, pulled out his clean clothes and stuffed them into his pack. His gaze was filled with pain and anger when he looked up at her.

Katarina almost burst out laughing at the mess she was in. "I didn't realize we'd reached that stage in *our* relationship."

"Do you expect me to leave without a fight?"

"Yes, I do. Ron didn't even ask me, he just blurted it out. I need time to explain." She waited for a reply that didn't come. "After two years, I think he deserves that much." She took hold of Alex's arm, and he pulled away. "We can talk later, can't we?"

He looked into her eyes, then shook his head and turned to leave. "I have to go."

"Please try to understand, Alex," she said, following him up the stairs. "This isn't easy for me."

Alex stopped at the top and waited for her to catch up. He lowered his voice and whispered into her ear. "Take all the time you want—just don't expect me to congratulate you and Ron. As you may have noticed, I'm not a good actor."

Alex gave her a quick kiss on the cheek, then left.

Ron watched Alex storm out the front door. "What was that all about?" He laughed.

Katarina felt her confidence waver. *"Never will I leave you, never will I forsake you." Thank You, Father, for being here with me.* She took a deep breath. "Ron, we need to talk." She motioned for him to sit down.

He took her hand in his and pulled her onto the sofa with him. "First, I want to see what this looks like on your finger. We can discuss the business later." He took the ring and slid it onto her finger easily, as it was way too large.

"There's no need to discuss business, Ron," she

said gently. Tears formed. "This isn't about Kat's Kreations."

"I'm sorry about my insensitive remark about the dolls, darling."

"That doesn't matter any longer."

"What do you mean? Didn't you accept the offer? You know you'll never get an offer like this again."

She shrugged. "Maybe not."

"What's going on? It's exactly as we planned."

"I thought a deal like this would make me happy. But to be honest, I've been depressed by the prospect ever since I received the call."

Ron continued to quote statistics to her.

"Ron, stop. This isn't what I need to talk to you about. I—" she took the ring and handed it back to Ron "—can't marry you."

His mouth fell open. "I should have known. All these years you've been afraid of being abandoned—and now you're the one leaving. Does that make you feel better somehow?"

"N-no," she stammered. "No, it doesn't. I'm sorry, Ron. I've prayed about this, and...I felt secure with you, but the love and passion to be together just wasn't there. You have to agree with that much. Our Father wants the best for both of us. We just aren't the best for each other. I'm very sorry."

"I'm sorry, too." He looked at his watch. "Well, now you've made me late to meet my parents. Good luck, Katarina. I hope you and what's-his-name find all the passion and happiness you can stand before it all goes up in smoke.''

Katarina chuckled, unsure the man had a clue what he'd just said. ''I hope so, too. And I pray you'll find the same happiness one day, Ron.''

He left, and the emptiness and fear set in. She'd just tossed a lifetime of caution aside in faith that her heavenly Father had a perfect path planned. Katarina took a deep breath. *I did it, Lord...Father...my Father. I couldn't have done it without You.*

Katarina changed back into jeans and a tank top with a denim shirt over it, then called Emily and Kevin. She packed a small bag while they talked.

''What happened?'' Emily asked Kevin to pick up the other extension.

She shrugged. ''Ron wasn't happy, but he wasn't totally shocked that I broke up with him. How could I explain that I think I'm in love with a man I haven't even kissed yet?''

Kevin laughed. ''Not even a kiss, huh?''

Emily cut Kevin's comment short. ''I think it's terribly romantic.''

''Kevin?'' Katarina smiled with nervous energy. ''Do you know where Alex went? Someplace called Bear Creek, maybe?''

''Somewhere northwest of Rustic, I think, but surely you aren't thinking of going there?'' Kevin's voice made it sound as if she was out to hurt the man.

Katarina couldn't erase the pain she'd seen in

Alex's expression before he left. "You don't understand. I asked him to leave. I only felt that I owed it to Ron to let him down without the humiliation of facing the man who has won my heart instead." She shrugged. "I need Alex to know that there's someone waiting for him when the fire is out."

Chapter Twenty

Katarina ignored Kevin's warning that finding Alex would be like looking for a needle in a haystack. She couldn't allow any shadow of doubt to stop her. A quick call to Greg Johannsen gave her a general vicinity to start looking for Alex.

Three hours later, Katarina saw a television-station vehicle turn onto a dirt road. She followed, taking a chance that they were going to the base camp for a live report on the five-o'clock news. Ten miles later, she pulled into a field of smashed and crumpled buffalo grass behind the reporters and found a place to park. Fear kept her inside her own van as she watched the organized commotion. Men and women wearing green pants and yellow shirts loaded boxes onto buses and stuffed their belongings into packs similar to Alex's. The news crew rushed to set up for the telecast. Suddenly the doubt she'd kept at bay for the better part of the drive attacked with full force.

Was she making more of Alex's interest than was really there? Was Alex the man she'd waited a lifetime for? What if she had walked away from Ron to find out that she and Alex were truly nothing more than fire and ice?

She looked around again. *There must be fifty people out there, all dressed alike. Searching the entire camp for one man is hopeless.* Giving in to her fear, she started the ignition and eased forward to leave. A red four-wheel-drive truck caught her eye.

Father, if this is Your will, let me find Alex before it's too late.

Katarina turned the key. Hesitantly she got out and wandered. Watching. Searching. Hoping.

The air smelled as if she'd stuck her head in a fireplace. She swallowed hard, forcing away the nausea. Katarina ignored the urge to cough. She shut out everything but finding the man she'd grown to love. She walked faster, scanning each identically dressed person, hoping one of them would be Alex. Hoping she hadn't already missed him. She didn't see anyone fitting the description of tall, lean and irresistible.

"May I help you?" one of the firefighters asked.

"I'm looking for Alex Mac—"

"Mac's on the other side of this bus. You just barely caught him. They're ready to head out."

Katarina pivoted and took a step, then turned to

thank the man, but the firefighter was already on his way. Katarina stepped around the back of the bus and ran right into Alex. Suddenly she was terrified. What had she done, following him here?

"Katarina? What? H-how..." he stammered, a look of absolute shock on his face. "How did you ever find me?"

Her heart thumped uncomfortably. Was he unhappy to see her?

Behind him, the bus started, and smoke billowed off the mountain. Katarina felt her heart race. "Greg Johannsen gave me the general directions. But I followed that television van here, actually."

"Load up, we're out of here!" the man at the front of the yellow school bus yelled, paying her no attention.

Alex backed up hesitantly, following orders in slow motion. "I want you to go home, Katarina. This smoke isn't good for your lungs. I want to know you're okay."

She was torn. "I'll be here. Waiting for you."

"Go home." He slung a pack over his shoulder and took a backward step onto the bus.

Katarina watched as the bus pulled away. *No, Alex. I will not go home.* She'd come too far to lose him now.

A few miles away Katarina found a small dude ranch with cabins to rent. She called Emily, picked up a few groceries at a nearby store and prepared herself to wait the fire out. She checked at the fire camp the next morning to see if Alex had come back with the rest of the crew.

Katarina had just missed Alex this time. He'd jumped into a neighboring fire as soon as he'd returned to the camp. How anyone kept track of who was where in this chaos was beyond her. Throughout the day, Katarina volunteered to help prepare meals and box lunches in the mess tent, keeping a silent vigil, watching and wondering where Alex could be, what he was thinking and how soon he would finish here. Finally the sunset turned to night. The fire left an eerie red glow on the horizon. She watched, mesmerized. *Lord, keep Alex safe.* Katarina returned to the cabin and went to bed. She tossed and turned, but finally exhaustion won.

Alex had been on the line for twenty-four hours straight before they had the fire contained. In a hurry to get back to camp, they crammed all the gear and groundpounders onto one bus. After a short break for just a few hours of sleep, they would join another crew of hotshots on the main fire. Not even exhaustion would stop him from calling Katarina before he took a nap.

He couldn't believe she had come here, or their continued lousy timing in missing each other. *One of these days, Lord, I'm going to catch up with that woman long enough to tell her how much I love her.*

They had demobilized at first light. He hadn't slept at all last night and the bus ride was too bumpy.

to catch any shut-eye. They pulled into the camp and discovered they were tearing down. The fire had taken a turn and was heading straight for them. Alex immediately went to his truck and dialed the house on his cellular phone.

No answer.

He left a message and called Emily.

"What do you mean, she's still here?" He looked frantically around for her van. "She's not here. They ordered this area to evacuate. Where was she staying?"

He ran through the camp, asking if anyone had seen Katarina. "Not since last night," said a woman. "She helped clean up after supper, then disappeared. Aren't you going to go out with your crew? They're leaving in ten minutes."

"I can't. Tell Tom I'm headed up the canyon. Katarina is staying at the Blue Mountain Dude Ranch. I'm going looking for her."

"Stay safe."

Alex ignored the makeshift driveway and drove across the pasture to the road. He hit the shallow ditch too fast, and bounced up onto the road, then rounded the bend. A finger of fire had already eaten every ponderosa in the ravine and jumped the river like a famished monster. With the current winds, not even the road was going to act as a firebreak. He could see the sign for the dude ranch ahead. A snag fell across the road, threatening to continue the feast on the little one-room cabins tucked in the midst of the dry brush—prime fire fuel.

Avoiding the flames, Alex four-wheeled over the log, hoping to break it apart before it had a chance to ignite the dry tinder on the other side of the road. The torch was solid. He called the base and reported the progress of the fire, requested a helitack on the cabins, then turned into the ranch in search of Katarina. Cabins were tucked single file in among aspen and pine for half a mile between the road and the south fork of the river.

On a final lap back toward the approaching fire, Alex four-wheeled behind the cabins. His heart raced when he saw her van parked between two cabins, and the flames lapping at the logs on one of them. He blared his horn, then stopped and jumped out of the cab and hit the ground running. "Katarina!" He pounded on the door, then turned the knob. The burning cabin was empty. He ran to the next one.

The door was locked. He kicked at it, but the solid wood door didn't budge. "They sure don't make them like this anymore."

Sparks popped. Wind blew hot and furious. Flames licked the side of her cabin.

Alex pulled his Pulaski from the back of his truck and sliced the doorknob off with one swing. "Katarina!"

Her willowy body lay on the bed in blissful slumber, oblivious to the danger. The fire popped and roared, angry and hungry. "Kat, wake up." He lifted her into his arms, covers and all.

She let out a small protest, then gasped. "Alex?"

Sleepy eyes popped open as he rushed out the door. A spray of water blasted them, as his crew kept the fire away with a garden hose.

"Get out of here, Mac. A helitack is on the way to make a water drop."

Katarina squirmed out of the blankets as she crawled into his truck ahead of him. He gunned the engine and drove away. "Didn't you hear about the evacuation?"

"No one said anything. That must be why the place was deserted last night." She straightened her wet T-shirt and pulled off her muddy socks.

"Didn't you hear the fire, or the wind?"

She shook her head. He couldn't tell if she was crying or if it was simply water dripping from her hair. "I was so tired last night, I took out my hearing aid and tried to sleep. I set the alarm to be at the base in time to help with breakfast."

"The fire probably knocked out the electricity."

She looked at her watch, then back at the fire. "Oh my. I did oversleep. What about my van and other things? My hearing aid is on the table next to the bed."

Alex paused. "We can't take a chance of getting caught in the cabin. If the helitack works, we'll go back. Not before." From a mile down the road they watched the helicopter approach, an orange bucket dangling beneath it. After the helicopter doused the area with the spray of water, they were able to return to the cabin for Katarina's things.

Alex led the way back to the fire base, his gaze glued to his rearview mirrors to make sure she stayed close behind. As soon as she stepped from her van, Alex took Katarina into his arms and put his mouth close to her left ear. "I have to go, Kat. Before I do, I want you to know how much I love you."

"I love you," she whispered back. Their lips met for the first time, and he felt buffeted by the winds of a savage harmony. She pressed her hands on his chest, and reluctantly they parted. The love he saw in her eyes sent his spirits soaring. "It's going to be okay, Alex. We can work it all out later. Go. Just know you have someone waiting for you when the fire's out."

He looked at her. She was smudged with soot, yet her cheeks were pink, and the smile on her face was as wide as his own.

"Mac, let's go," another fireman called to Alex.

"I'll be back, Katarina."

"I love you, Alex."

They contained the fire in two days and Alex stepped off that bus for the last time without another question or regret. He'd faced his fears and closed that book behind him.

As she'd promised, Katarina was waiting for him,

looking as bright and cheery as sunshine. Just the sight of her youthful radiance made him feel ten years younger. Even though he was filthy from four days on the fire, with their first kiss still fresh in his memory, Katarina's silent pleading invitation for another was too hard to resist.

Katarina melted into his embrace, and he realized immediately that his feelings for her were intensifying way too quickly. They had a lot to talk about; just as soon as he cleaned up.

Later, over supper at a restaurant in town, Alex told her he didn't plan to finish out the fire season.

"You don't have to give up fire fighting for me," Katarina insisted, tears welling in her eyes.

He pulled her closer and touched his forehead to hers. "I'm not giving anything up, Kat. I'm moving on, to the family I ran away from. To the love God planned for us. On to the family I hope we'll have one day." He kissed her gently, lingering, savoring every moment. "I don't want to miss one more day with you." He felt the heat of her blush on his hand. Or was it simply his imagination?

"Won't you miss the excitement and adventure?"

"Surely you jest...." He shook his head. "I don't think we'll be lacking in either."

Katarina's tears were replaced with a warm glow. Alex liked to think it was a result of the love God had helped them find in each other.

He turned, looking back at his buddies behind him. Country-and-western music crooned in the background. "You aren't taking the fire out of me, Kat, you've given it back." Despite the lack of privacy and romantic atmosphere, Alex knelt beside Katarina. "I promised I wouldn't make it easy for you to walk away, Katarina. And I'd love to spend every day of the rest of my life keeping that promise."

For a moment he'd seen fear in her eyes, but only for an instant. She leaned close and whispered in his ear, "Did you just propose?"

He chuckled, then kissed her. "I sure did. You turned your hearing aid off again, huh?" He didn't mind the excuse to nuzzle next to her and repeat his proposal. He waited for an answer.

"I thought you'd never ask," she said, grinning mischievously.

Now he was the puzzled one. "Exactly how long have you been waiting?"

"I've been dreaming of this since the day I first met you."

Alex shook his head. "And to think I wasted all this time worrying about you and the Boy Scout."

Katarina pressed her lips to his. "He never stood a chance after sparks began to fly between us."

"And that took all of ten seconds."

"Ten seconds to light, an eternity to put out."

He smiled. "Maybe I'm not ready to retire from fire fighting after all."

Chapter Twenty-One

"You're what?" Emily and Kevin echoed. Katarina and Alex had met their sister and brother for lunch the next day when they arrived in town.

Alex laughed. "We're engaged. Getting married. You know—going to the chapel and we're..."

Kevin held up his hands, motioning for Alex to stop. "I get it, I get it. Don't sing."

Despite Alex's inability to carry a tune, Katarina leaned closer and smiled. "I kind of liked it. You can serenade me anytime. I can see it now, you in the loft..."

Alex rested his hand on Katarina's shoulder. "I plan to move out of the house until after the wedding."

Katarina's eyebrows arched up and her mouth fell open. "What?"

He'd meant to tell her that last night, but with all

the commotion at the restaurant after he'd proposed, Alex had barely seen his fiancée. The women fire-fighters had taken it upon themselves to drag Katarina away after dinner.

"It's totally different now, Katarina."

She lowered her voice. "Yesterday it was okay that we shared a house, and today it's suddenly different?"

"When I left," he countered, "we weren't dating. It wasn't easy then, and I don't expect it'll be any easier to resist temptation now."

Emily smiled. "I'm so happy for you two. When I saw Alex pulling you out from under the table at the wedding, I knew this day would come. Have you set a date?"

Alex and Katarina glanced toward each other. "How about February?" Alex offered. "We should be done with the lodge by then. I might be able to talk the boss into a few days off for a honeymoon."

Kevin cleared his throat.

"I hate to throw a kink into your plans, but February might be cutting it close. We're expecting…"

Before he could say another word, Katarina let out a squeal, flew to her sister's side and gave her a hug. "Oh, Emmy. A baby! This is so exciting."

The room burst into a round of applause. "Well, it should be around the entire medical community by the end of the day," Emily muttered with a smile.

Alex shook his brother's hand. "Congratulations,

Kevin. You've waited a long time for a family. I couldn't be happier for you.''

Kevin slapped his brother's shoulder. "Likewise. I hate to say I told you so, but..."

Katarina slid back into the booth next to Alex and gave him a puzzled look. "What's this all about?"

Alex wrapped his arm around her shoulder and kissed her forehead. "After I caught the garter, Kevin suggested I just give in right away. Seems to have become a family tradition."

Emily laughed. "So I guess Adam and Lisa had better watch out, huh?"

There was a pause around the table. "Lisa and Adam." Katarina smiled. "Now, that's an idea."

Kevin and Alex shared a glance and laughed aloud. "You're talking about Adam. The eternal bachelor. No way are you going to set those two up."

Kevin nodded in agreement with his brother's comment. "Lisa's always on the road. And Adam doesn't travel. Besides that, two Berthoff-MacIntyre marriages in the family should be sufficient, don't you think? I mean, if there's any sort of disagreement..."

Emily had a mischievous grin. "You afraid the sisters might take sides?"

"Or stage some sort of boycott?" Katarina continued.

Alex laughed. "This is a no-win argument, Kevin. If you're not careful, you and I are going to be finding an apartment together. If Kat and Emmy think they can mix oil and water, they have my blessing." He leaned close to Katarina, then paused, as if waiting for permission to kiss her.

Katarina studied him freely. She rather liked looking at Alex without feeling guilty or as if she was being "caught" doing so. "You're serious, aren't you?"

"I've never been more content in my life. Why wouldn't I want Adam to find the same happiness? Just don't set your hopes too high. I don't want you to be disappointed." He looked at his watch. "I hate to leave so soon, but I should get to work." He leaned over and kissed Katarina. "I'll see you tonight."

Katarina spent the afternoon catching up on her inventory and designs, then began preparations for the huge show next weekend. Maybe Alex would like to come with her, she thought. There were so many things to talk about with him when he came home from work. She smiled. *When he came home from work.* That sounded so nice. Disappointment that Alex would be moving out threatened to cast a shadow over the day, yet she reminded herself that it wouldn't be for long. Then they'd have forever together.

While Alex doubted there were many things they hadn't covered at some point in their conversations this summer, he wanted to know everything about the woman with whom he planned to spend the rest of his life.

They hadn't even had a chance to discuss her decision about Unique Designs, or his desire to become a full partner with Kevin. Would she want him to sign some prenuptial agreement, as she had planned with Ron? Did she want children? If so, how many? Suddenly he felt as if he was walking into some business meeting for negotiations.

He realized the mountain he'd asked God to help him move had been totally blown out of the way all in one overwhelming blast. Had he been too eager? Too quick to propose? Katarina had been skittish about marriage from the day he'd met her. Why in the world hadn't he waited a month or two before popping the question? If they were so right for each other, the answer would be the same now or later.

He saw no sign of Katarina when he pulled into the driveway. Alex took a deep breath and let it out. "Father, You've brought me this far, please don't let me blow it now." He walked up the steps, discouraged to find an envelope with his name on it taped to the storm door.

A heart-shaped note inside read, "Meet me in the gazebo." Katarina signed it with a heart. "Your blissfully happy fiancée."

The evening sun bathed the room with a warm glow. Alex passed through the house and walked out to the gazebo. His mouth fell open. She'd strung white twinkle lights along the top of the lattice and set a table inside.

"I thought this was the perfect place to start our relationship together—" she walked up the steps and wrapped her arms around his waist from behind "—since this is where you found me that first night after you moved in."

"You mean the night you were trying to hide from me?" Alex loosened her hands and turned within her embrace.

She laughed. "It used to work with Mom."

He pulled her close and wrapped his arms around her waist. "Nice try. I wanted to take you out to dinner tonight, but it looks like you already have plans."

"I do. I'm meeting my fiancé here." He felt her smile grow. "I love the way that sounds, by the way." Soft music filled the air.

He brushed his lips along hers. "I like hearing you say it. I worried that I rushed into the proposal."

She didn't respond.

Alex backed away. "If you want more time to decide, I'll understand."

"Do you want more time?" A spark of fear flashed in her eyes.

"No." He hesitated. "I realize there are a lot of things we should discuss...."

Katarina nodded. "And a lot of time to talk about them. The rest of the meal is ready. Why don't we grill the salmon while we start?"

"How did you know I love salmon?"

"I didn't. I just hoped you would, since I do. I wanted to fix something nice for our first official date."

Salmon was just one of the many similarities they discovered in the course of their evening. They both felt it important to take their time moving on to marriage, since they hadn't really dated yet. While they were sympathetic to Emily's pregnancy, they hesitated to cut their engagement too much shorter, and definitely didn't want to wait until after the baby came.

Four children fit their image of the "dream family," but both agreed that was up for discussion.

Alex supported Katarina's decision to continue running her business independently, and was happy when she admitted the prenuptial idea belonged to Ron.

The next Sunday morning they went to church together for the first time as a couple and wasted no time making an appointment to start premarriage meetings with the pastor. Alex found a small attic apartment to stay in until they found a house to buy.

The following weekend, Alex joined Katarina at her doll show, which ended up bringing in two more monthly orders, and her first order for children's dolls.

After the show, Alex took her to a jewelry store. She looked at the three rings on the velvet display. "I just can't decide. I'd like something similar to these. You choose." She snuggled close.

When they finished shopping, Alex pulled into a nice restaurant. After they ordered, he pulled a box from his pocket and opened it before her. Her crystal-blue eyes opened wide. As he spoke, her gaze locked with his. "Katarina, I want you to wear this ring as a token of my vow to love and cherish you for the rest of my life."

"Oh, Alex." She bit her lip to stifle the outcry of delight. "I didn't see this ring. It's beautiful." She touched the pale green and pink tone gold leaves surrounding the diamond.

He took the delicate gold solitaire from the box, kissed the ring, then placed it on her finger and kissed it again.

"I still can't quite believe this. It's all happened so quickly. All these years I thought this day would never happen. Now I know why love always seemed to pass me by. I was waiting for you." The tenderness in her voice touched him deeply. It was something he couldn't begin to understand, let alone explain. Falling in love with Katarina caught him off guard, yet left his heart at peace. Life together would be one joyful adventure after another.

"And I for you, love."

Chapter Twenty-Two

Katarina and Alex started planning an early January wedding, but by the end of September they'd moved it up to December to accommodate family schedules.

For most of the week prior to the wedding, Katarina, her mother and sisters finalized plans arranging flowers and made final adjustments to their gowns. Katarina sewed pearls to the lace on her wedding dress. Emily's emerald-green rayon crinkle dress had grown increasingly tight since she'd tried it on just a week ago.

Katarina patted her sister's expanding tummy. "Emily, I love this baby with all my heart, but could you please tell it to stop growing for two more days? I'm nearly out of fabric here."

"Sure, no problem." Emily smiled. "I can't believe you, Kat. Choosing a style and fabric with my pregnancy in mind. Not to mention waiting to sew it together until the week of the wedding.''

"I think you did a beautiful job, sis. As usual." Lisa twirled around, and the tea-length skirt swirled around her long legs. "What do you think?"

"Show-off," Emily muttered. "I don't think I'll ever be thin again."

"You look radiant, Emily. Trust me, it's worth every ounce, even if you never lose it," their mother said.

Katarina could see that the confession shocked all three sisters. Naomi Berthoff had had a difficult time as a single mother and rarely ever talked positively about their childhood.

"I was afraid you were making the same mistake I did with your father, Katarina," Naomi said solemnly.

Katarina was silent. Did she really have to wait until the day before her wedding? After five months, including their Thanksgiving visit, Katarina would have thought her mother could have chosen a better time to criticize her choice of husband. "Mother…"

"I never told any of you girls. We were married two weeks after we met. Karl was charming, and handsome, and swept me off my feet." Naomi seemed to drift into her own world. Emily and Lisa looked at each other, then at Kat. "Alex—" Naomi paused to wipe her teary eyes "—is everything I could have ever hoped for in a husband for you,

Katarina. He adores you, and it's obvious that you feel the same. I've never seen you so at peace.''

Relief washed over Katarina, and she embraced her mother. ''Thank you, Mom. Alex and I are very happy.'' Kat hesitated. No one had broached this subject for at least fifteen years. Each birthday, graduation and family wedding, Katarina had hoped her father would magically reappear and everything would return to normal. Each time, she dreamed of welcoming him home with open arms. Of pushing the anger and hurt aside. ''Mamma, why did Daddy leave without even saying goodbye?''

Her mother touched Katarina's cheek and looked her in the eyes. ''Are you sure you want to talk about this now, right before your wedding?''

Kat nodded. ''I need to know.''

Naomi wrapped her arm around Katarina and took Lisa's hand. ''Your father and I simply didn't know each other well enough before we married, honey. In our own way, we tried to find that magical feeling that had brought us together, but I realize now, there was never any love.'' Her mother let out a deep breath. ''I woke up one morning and accepted the truth. I couldn't live with it any longer.''

Her mother took a lengthy pause. ''When he left that night, I told him not to bother coming back.'' Not a tear dropped from her mother's eyes. ''Of course, we'd been through the same argument so many times, I didn't really mean it at the time. He took me seriously.''

Despite her mother's mistakes, Katarina admired her. Naomi Berthoff had become a strong, determined woman because of what her father had done.

Her mother hugged each daughter, and Katarina wept for only a few minutes after finally learning the truth. That in itself made moving on easier. Alex was right—no matter what Karl Berthoff had done, she would always have her heavenly Father.

Fresh holly, pink and white poinsettias, and cranberry candles with white satin bows decorated the candelabras at the altar. Hurricane lamps adorned each pew, lighting the sanctuary with a soft glow. Katarina watched Emily, then Lisa disappear through the double doors. They closed again so she could take her place.

"You look ravishing, sweetie. That's one fine man you're marrying."

Katarina's heart swelled with pride. "Thanks, Grandpa. I'm so glad you felt up to coming."

"I was so disappointed I couldn't come to Emily's wedding. I wasn't about to miss another. Are we ready?"

She nodded. As if on cue, the wedding march began. Her grandfather's roughened hand patted hers and the doors opened. The congregation blocked her view of her husband-to-be. Halfway down the aisle, their eyes met. Alex's entire face lit up when he first saw her. Katarina, chilly from a bad case of the jitters and the howling blizzard outside, felt the chill melt away inch by inch under her groom's admiring gaze.

The tails of Alex's tux emphasized his broad shoulders, slim hips and long legs, making him even more attractive than ever. He accepted her hand from her grandfather, then helped her up the step to the pastor.

Katarina glanced at the cross above the altar and felt as if she'd been anointed with His love and assurance. *Thank you, Father.* As if Alex was reading her mind, he squeezed her hand. Kat looked at him with dreamy eyes, melting away the years of loneliness and longing. Never had any decision felt so right.

"'Delight thyself in the Lord and He shall give you desires of thine heart. Commit thy way unto the Lord, trust in Him and He shall bring it to pass.' During our visits, Alex and Katarina shared this verse with me as a testament of their relationship." The pastor continued to speak about the beauty of the bond of marriage created by Him for His glory.

Katarina had taken a leap of faith opening her soul to Him, leaving the security of the familiar for the unknown realm of seeking God's will.

Alex felt his voice choke with emotion as he recited his vows to love, honor and cherish Katarina. Adam handed him the ring, and he slid it onto his bride's long, delicate finger. "With this ring, I thee wed."

He recalled her proclamation that she would be

waiting for him when the fire was out. He had news for his bride. That fire would *never* go out. Her blond hair shimmered in the candlelight. Joy flickered in her blue eyes. Her icy hands were now warm within his own gentle grasp.

As Katarina finished her vows, kissed his ring and placed the gold band on his finger, Alex anticipated showing her just how much he cherished the love she entrusted to him.

"You may kiss your bride." Alex lifted the veil covering her porcelain face and wrapped his arms securely around her. "I love you, Katarina." The intimacy of their kiss reached a new level as God joined their hearts in peaceful harmony.

Merely an hour later, the severity of the storm forced them to bring the festivities to an abrupt end. Katarina changed quickly and looked down the wide stairs to the exit. Katarina and Alex descended the stairs and stopped halfway. She spotted the youngest MacIntyre brother near the doorway and tried to figure out how to get Lisa to catch the bouquet and Adam to catch the garter as Kevin and Emily, and she and Alex, had done.

Thus far, they'd had no luck whatsoever in setting the two of them up together. "Do not be anxious about anything, but in everything, by prayer and petition, with thanksgiving, present your requests to God." *Okay, Father. Lisa and Adam are in Your hands.*

Katarina turned, closed her eyes and tossed the

bouquet. She spun around to watch it catch on the crystal chandelier in front of the door. Her heart deflated. "Alex, we have to get it."

Laughter bubbled throughout the entryway.

"This isn't a tree, Kat. That chandelier is a good twenty feet from the ground. There's no way to retrieve it without risking bodily harm, for man or crystal. Afraid the bouquet won this time."

Tiny champagne-colored bubbles floated up the stairs as someone opened the door for Alex and Katarina to exit. "Everyone's waiting on us to leave so they can get home."

She looked up again, then to Adam and Lisa before finally parading down the stairs. The guests followed them out the door as the freshly fallen snow swirled as if in a winter wonderland.

"Are you going to tell me where we're staying?"

He looked up into the blizzard, hugging her close by his side. "Luckily, you have an impatient husband. I didn't want to spend our wedding night on the road, so I reserved the honeymoon suite at a hotel across town. But at this rate, our flight to Hawaii may have to wait another day or two."

"Hawaii? Alex!" He opened the door and helped her climb into the truck. "How did you manage that on such short notice?"

He smiled. "That's only the beginning, Katarina. Nothing is impossible when you hand the control to Him."

*　　*　　*　　*　　*

Dear Reader,

Some of you may have read *Second Time Around* and fallen in love with Katarina and Alex just as I did. When I finished writing Emily and Kevin's story, I realized there was more to this extraordinary story of God's everlasting love than one book could ever tell. I wondered how the other two sisters, Katarina and Lisa, would handle the pain of their father's abandonment, and how it would mold not only their earthly lives, but their spiritual lives, as well.

And these MacIntyre men—they're pretty special, too. Alex, the daring smoke jumper, Kevin, the charming builder and Adam, the rugged cowboy, are all men of integrity. Men you can count to steal your heart, mold it and give you one incredible ride in the process.

I hope you enjoy this series of two incredible families and how God has brought them together through three totally unique love stories that draw on the individual needs and personalities of each couple. We have all been created in His image, with faults, weaknesses and special gifts that are as unique as our own fingerprints.

I love to hear from my readers. Please write to me at P.O. Box 5021, Greeley, CO, 80632-0021.

Carol Steward

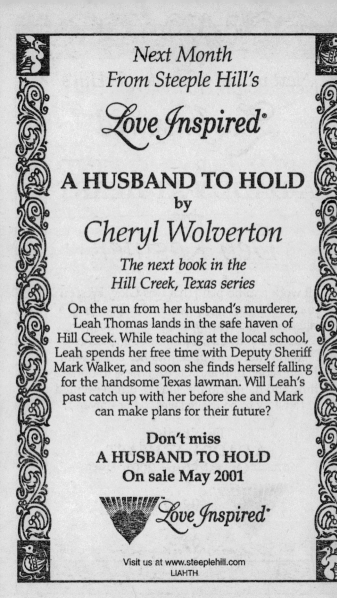

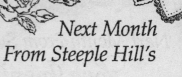